For Services to Medicine

Colin Douglas

Hutchinson

London Melbourne Sydney Auckland Johannesburg

By the same author

The Houseman's Tale
The Greatest Breakthrough since Lunchtime
Bleeders Come First
Wellies from the Queen
A Cure for Living

Hutchinson & Co. (Publishers) Ltd

An imprint of the Hutchinson Publishing Group

17–21 Conway Street, London W1P 6JD

Hutchinson Publishing Group (Australia) Pty Ltd
16–22 Church Street, Hawthorne, Melbourne, Victoria 3122

Hutchinson Group (NZ) Ltd
32–34 View Road, PO Box 40–086, Glenfield, Auckland 10

Hutchinson Group (SA) Pty Ltd
PO Box 337, Bergvlei 2012, South Africa

First published 1985
© Colin Douglas 1985

Set in Compugraphic Baskerville by
Colset Private Ltd, Singapore

Printed and bound in Great Britain by Anchor Brendon Ltd,
Tiptree, Essex

British Library Cataloguing in Publication Data

Douglas, Colin
For Services to Medicine
I. Title
823'.914   PR6054.0825

ISBN 0 09 159540 1

PART ONE

'There seems to have been some mistake.' The woman looked at Campbell with distaste.

'Some mistake,' said the man.

'I'm sorry,' said Campbell. 'I was called to the ward and it took longer than I had expected.' A man had died who should not have died.

'I can understand that,' said the woman. 'But there still seems to have been some kind of mistake.'

The man looked as though he were about to speak. The woman silenced him with a small gesture. He began to pick his nose.

'We were expecting a lady doctor.' She reached across and pulled his hand down from his face.

He spoke again. 'A lady doctor.'

'A near genius, according to Dr Minto.'

'Well . . .' Campbell started, for the eighth or tenth time that week, to explain. The woman interrupted him. 'Dr Minto insisted we see her urgently and arranged it with the head of the Department of Neurology . . . And the woman's name was foreign. Cow something.'

'Jankowska,' said Campbell.

The woman looked at him suspiciously and sniffed. Seconds later the man sniffed too. 'That might have been it,' she said.

'Might have been it.'

'I see,' said Campbell. 'Will you come this way?'

He led them into one of the examination rooms and asked them to sit down, then went back to the reception desk to get the case folder which would at least tell him the man's name and date of birth. As he returned to the examination room he heard the woman's voice, insistent and indistinct, and the man's monosyllabic reply.

Campbell sat down at the desk. 'Mr Duke? Mr Ian Duke?'

The man smiled. The woman pursed her lips and said, 'I told you there'd been some mistake. Couldn't we just see the head of the department instead?'

'I'm sorry,' said Campbell. 'Not today. He's in Dundee, and he's not expected back here until tomorrow.'

'But it's urgent,' said the woman.

'I'm sorry,' said Campbell. 'It is Mr Duke, isn't it?'

The man nodded. His wife spoke. 'It's actually *Dr* Duke. We're medical, you see. We saw Dr Minto privately, in his rooms in Moray Place, and he said the person to see about this was . . . The doctor with the funny name. But if we can't see her obviously we'd like to see the head of the department . . . Dr . . .'

'Dr Brown?'

'Yes. Dr Brown.'

'Dr Brown isn't actually head of the department, but he's head of . . . this part of the department. The Neurobiology Unit.'

'Yes. That's who we should be seeing.'

'I'm afraid he's in Dundee for the rest of the day.'

The woman looked at Campbell with renewed distaste. 'Well,' she said, 'if there's no one else . . .'

Campbell smiled.

'It's really the drug we've come about,' said the woman. 'The new memory drug.'

'The new memory drug,' said the man.

The couple were perhaps in their early sixties, the woman well preserved, alert and anxious, the man reserved and sullen, his face a patient blank. Campbell glanced again at the inside cover of the case folder. Under the heading 'General Practitioner' there was a space. Under 'Occupation' was typed 'General Practitioner'.

2

The woman spoke again. 'You haven't introduced yourself, doctor.'

'Oh. Sorry. I'm Dr Campbell. I've just started here.'

Mrs Duke pursed her lips and was silent, as though vindicated in her worst suspicions. Campbell considered how to regain the initiative.

'Mrs Duke, it might be best if you and I discussed things. Dr Duke, I wonder if . . .'

'Ian,' said the woman. The man stood up. 'Wait outside.'

'Will he be all right?' Campbell asked when the man had left.

'He doesn't wander.'

Campbell sat down again and reached for pen and paper.

'I hope this is confidential.'

'Everything is.'

'Especially with us being medical. I mean, Ian and I obviously wish to avoid any professional embarrassment.'

'It's all right. Everything is kept strictly confidential. More so, if anything, than in other out-patient departments. So how did all this begin?'

There was a pause. Campbell put down his pen. The woman began to talk.

'He's a brilliant man, really. An Edinburgh graduate. He won prizes and he would have been a surgeon if things had turned out differently. As it was, the children came along and, of course, he put them first and went into practice, but a very well-established practice. You probably know it. Tansey Street. Dr McVittie's the senior partner . . . And the patients just worship Ian. They know he's really far too brilliant to be doing what he's doing, and I think they appreciate that.'

'Mrs Duke . . .'

'I'm coming to how it started. It's just to let you understand what he was like before. He loves his work and he's still very good at it and I think we should be quite clear about that from the start . . . Are you sure there hasn't been some mistake? We saw Dr Minto, you know. In Moray Place. Privately. And he gave us a full hour and was wonderfully sympathetic and helpful. It just seems odd that he didn't arrange for us to see, you know, the top person.'

'Mrs Duke, I think Dr Brown was expecting to be in the Unit this afternoon and was called away to Dundee at very short notice. If you'd like to make another appointment I'm sure he'd be very happy to see you. But he is the director of a very big multicentre trial and his duties quite often . . .'

'All right.'

'So can we go back to the beginning? How this all started.'

'It was probably overwork. And strain.'

'Could you explain that a bit more? The things you began to notice first . . .'

'He's very methodical, you know. Which is wonderful for general practice because you look after people, really look after them, for years and years.'

'So what did you notice?'

'Well, nothing very sudden. I mean he doesn't make mistakes or anything. Really, it was something with the family. He's a wonderful father, and grandfather too, of course, and I suppose the very first thing I noticed was when he forgot our oldest grandson's birthday. I'd remembered, of course, and had done the card, and he picked it up and said, "Who's Duncan?" To be honest, I thought he was joking.'

'I see.'

'Sometimes, of course, it's just preoccupation, I think. He forgets things, just little things, because he's worrying about something more important, a difficult case maybe. He's so terribly conscientious. Did I tell you that?'

'Sort of . . . Mrs Duke, have there ever been any difficulties at work? Problems about forgetting appointments or even, for example, with . . . things to do with patients?'

'Like I said, he's terribly methodical. And we've got a wonderful receptionist. A real gem. Knows all the patients inside out. And one of the nicest things about general practice is that most of it is really just keeping things ticking over. Routine things . . . Like . . .'

'What?'

'Repeat prescriptions, sick lines, that sort of thing.'

'And was he . . . is he managing the non-routine things all right too?'

'What?'

4

'Well . . . house calls, for example.'

The woman laughed. 'House calls? There's really hardly any demand for them, nowadays, in modern practice. Twenty years ago, yes, he loved them. But it's different now. And besides, we've been very lucky in our trainees.'

'And is he managing nights on duty all right?'

She smiled patiently. 'Ian's a fairly senior partner. And I don't know how much you know about general practice, Dr . . . Dr . . .'

'Campbell.'

'Dr Campbell. But between the trainees and the deputizing service there really isn't an awful lot of night work left for the senior men to do.'

'But . . .?'

'Well, when I say he manages night calls, it hasn't actually been necessary for a year or two. We still do afternoons though. And, of course, having trained as a nurse myself I can cope with an awful lot of the usual things that happen. Over the telephone, of course.'

'I see.'

Mrs Duke took out a handkerchief. Her hand was shaking. She smiled again, fiercely, at Campbell. 'Sometimes I think you hospital doctors don't have any real idea what it's like, outside your ivory towers.'

Campbell smiled back. 'I'm sure you're right. So what exactly's been the trouble, Mrs Duke? What made you think it might be a good idea to see Dr Minto?'

'I told you. His memory. He's forgetting things. And we saw a thing in the *Scotsman* about the new memory drug. I actually thought Dr Minto would just give it to us there and then. But it seems he thought it would be best to refer us up to this place.'

Campbell weighed his words. 'Probably better this way. I mean no criticism of Dr Minto, but . . .'

A short sharp female scream rang down the corridor outside. Before Campbell could move Mrs Duke was on her feet and at the door.

'Ian!'

She walked quickly back to the reception desk.

'Ian! That's enough!'

5

Dr Duke was standing facing the receptionist at the desk, with his back to his wife and Campbell.

'That's enough of that, Ian! Put it away. Put it away this minute or I'll be very, very angry.'

She took her husband by the arm, then turned to the receptionist, who was now flustered rather than alarmed. 'He's all right, dear. He's all right really. He wouldn't lay a finger on you. It's just his way of doing things. Ian!'

Awkwardly Dr Duke adjusted his clothing. His wife stooped to help him, talking over her shoulder to the receptionist. 'He's just sometimes a little . . . outgoing. Means well, of course, and it doesn't mean he doesn't like you . . . I expect in a clinic like this you get quite a lot of that sort of thing.'

The girl at the desk smiled and went on with her typing. Campbell introduced himself to Dr Duke and asked him to come along to the examination room.

'Shall I come with you, Dr Campbell?' his wife asked.

'No thanks, Mrs Duke. But if you don't mind waiting I'd like to see you again before you go.'

Mrs Duke smiled and nodded. Dr Duke padded contentedly down the corridor towards the examination room, with Campbell steering him by the elbow.

That incident over, and away from his wife, Dr Duke seemed to brighten a little. He sat in the examination room looking round and smiling. Campbell began the interview. 'Dr Duke . . . can you tell me what year you were born?'

'Nineteen eighteen. The year the war ended.'

'And how old are you now?'

'Well, I graduated from Edinburgh in nineteen forty-one and went straight into the army. Wonderful life for a young doctor.'

'I'm sure,' said Campbell. 'And what age are you now?'

'And then went straight into practice when the war ended. North Shields. Wonderful people. But . . . But . . . But what's her name . . . my wife really wanted to get back to Edinburgh. So I'm stuck with that silly old bugger McVittie 'til death do us part.'

'Dr Duke, Dr Minto has asked if we could do anything about your memory.'

6

'What?'

'Your memory.'

'Nothing wrong with my memory. Can you remember your anatomy, lad? Not too many of you young fellows can. Name the arteries of the circle of Willis? Eh? Not too many of you young chaps can, you know. The circle of Willis lies in the cisterna interpeduncularis in the neighbourhood of the interpeduncular space. It is formed by the anterior communicating, the anterior cerebral, the posterior communicating and, of course . . . ah, the posterior cerebral and basilar arteries. Know that stuff? Reel it off like that? Eh? And I'm pretty fit too.'

Dr Duke got up from his chair and stood to attention for a moment, then, with his legs still straight, bent forward from the waist and laid his hands flat on the floor. He rose smiling. 'Most of you chaps can't even touch your toes.'

Campbell indicated that Dr Duke should sit down again. He did so. 'Regular exercise. Keep your eye on the ball. And your elbow off the bar. And your powder dry. Rules for a healthy life. And your working parts clean and lightly oiled.'

'Yes, I'm sure. And how about your memory? I was wondering . . .'

'Wonder away. It's wonderful to behold. Wander wonderingly in the circle of Willis. Know your anatomy, eh? And I keep pretty fit too.'

Dr Duke got up, stood straight, bent forward and once more put his hands flat on the floor. This time he laughed and said, 'Could you do that when you were my age, laddie?'

'I was going to ask that,' said Campbell. 'What age are you now?'

'I was born in nineteen eighteen. The year the war ended.'

'Yes, but to test your memory, can you tell me what age you are now?'

There was a longish pause. Campbell made the appropriate note on the test sheet then asked, 'And just to test your memory, can you tell me what year it is now?'

Dr Duke looked Campbell straight in the eye and said, 'If you don't know that yourself, laddie, you shouldn't be practising medicine.'

7

Campbell marked the test sheet once more. 'To test your memory, Dr Duke, I wonder if you could tell me what year it is now?'

Dr Duke looked round the room, then said, 'Where is she? That woman who was here? She knows all about that sort of thing. Trained as a nurse, silly bitch.'

So far Dr Duke had scored only one mark out of a possible three. Campbell went on down his list and asked who was the Prime Minister ('Major Attlee. A scholar and a gentleman. But unsound on things he doesn't understand, like medicine') and then who was on the throne ('New chap. With a stutter'). When pressed about the day of the week he again said, 'If you don't know that yourself, laddie, you shouldn't be practising medicine,' so that Campbell was compelled to speculate on what trainees were offered in the Tansey Street practice, other than large incentives to find their own way in medicine.

Perhaps whoever had devised the test sheet Campbell was using had never met anyone like Dr Duke. When asked to name ten towns, he got only as far as three, but used each as a peg for long anecdote and youthful biography. Asked for the names of ten kinds of flower, he dwelt on the merits of gardening as a hobby for doctors. After half an hour, though he remained cheerful, commanding and sometimes even amusing, he had scored less than ten points out of a possible fifty.

As he had said, he was physically fit. Campbell examined him quickly, concentrating, as the protocol directed, on looking for abnormalities of the nervous system. He tested Dr Duke's vision, pupil reactions, hearing and touch sensation, and then went methodically over the various reflexes in the schedule, ending by scratching the soles of the man's feet. The toes curled physiologically downwards. Dr Duke looked momentarily thoughtful, then said, 'That's another thing you laddies don't know nowadays. Who was Babinski?'

Had Campbell been asked that question in an exam, he would have confessed ignorance or perhaps, given genially postprandial examiners, chanced a bluff about the presumably nineteenth-century, presumably Russian neurologist who had first described the reflex just tested. It would be

8

interesting to know. 'I don't know. Who was he?'

'Some silly Russian bugger, I suppose,' said Dr Duke.

'I've finished now, thank you. You can put your clothes on.'

Dr Duke sat on the edge of the examination couch looking puzzled. Campbell handed him his shirt. He took it, played with the buttons for a while then put one foot into a sleeve. Campbell was about to ask a nurse to come and help, but thought better of it and asked Dr Duke to wait while he got Mrs Duke to rejoin them.

She was sitting in the waiting area, not reading a copy of *Scottish Field*, and got up when Campbell appeared.

'How is he?'

'Well, physically, as you know, he's very fit.'

'So you'll be able to help his memory?'

Campbell paused. Mrs Duke prompted him. 'The new memory drug. Aura something?'

'Well . . . it's not quite as straightforward as that. There are some more psychological tests, and other tests, including special X-rays, a CAT scan, actually, that perhaps can't be done for about a week. And there are blood tests too, to check his thyroid . . . That kind of thing.'

'And then he gets the drug?'

'Well, if the tests are as expected . . . Meantime, could you please help Dr Duke . . . with his clothes? And I'll try and arrange some of the tests then come back and we can talk about things.'

'Auragen. That's what it's called.'

'Yes.'

'So he can get it?'

'I'll get the tests together. Then I'll have to discuss things with Dr Brown.'

'So perhaps next week . . .?'

'Well, I'll try and get everything done as quickly as possible. And I'll have a word with Dr Brown as soon as he gets back. Probably first thing tomorrow.'

'Dr Brown. Is that Bobby Brown?'

'Yes.'

'We hadn't realized. We know him quite well.'

'Oh.'

9

'It's such a common name. But if it's Bobby Brown, we were sitting next to him at a dinner only last month. Something to do with a drug for Parkinson's.'

'Yes, probably. He's a senior lecturer in the Department of Neurology.'

'Short chap? Fair?'

'That's him.'

'I'm sure he'll want to do the best thing for Ian.'

'Of course.'

In the examination room Dr Duke was still wrestling with his shirt. His wife dressed him as Campbell started to write up his findings in the case folder, trying not to intrude. Mrs Duke finished by tightening her husband's tie with force and emphasis, then patted his hair and said, 'All right, darling? Dr Campbell? What about our next appointment?'

'Well, I thought that first we ought to have a talk about things. What's wrong and what . . .'

'I think I'll just ring Bobby about all this. Might be simplest,' said Mrs Duke.

'Might be simplest,' said her husband.

As they stood to go, the door opened and Dr Brown came in. Short and cheerful, and smelling strongly of a good lunch, he ignored Campbell and greeted the other two. 'Heather! Ian! How nice to see you again.'

Dr Duke smiled vacantly and shook the proffered hand. Mrs Duke glared at Campbell. Dr Brown beamed. 'Awfully glad to be able to help an old friend. Sorry not to be here earlier. I'd really meant to be here to start things off myself. I try to do all the initial assessments personally. So important in a project like this to get off to a good start with a rock-solid data base . . . And, of course, especially with a colleague, someone like yourself, Ian. I'm trying to think where we last met. One of these supper colloquium things? At the Comiston? Parotrim, wasn't it? Yes, grand stuff, we're using a great deal of it now. And, Ian, I'm delighted to be able to tell you that what Parotrim has done for Parkinson's disease, this new stuff is going to do for . . . your complaint, Ian. It's as good as that. Knowing that must be a great load off your mind, Heather, isn't it?'

10

Mrs Duke took her husband's hand. 'Hear that, Ian? Everything's going to be all right now with your memory.'

'Nothing wrong with my memory,' said Dr Duke.

Dr Brown laughed. 'Well, Ian, there certainly won't be three months from now. I'll just pop up to my office straight away and get your first month's tablets. No, Heather, it's no trouble . . . For a friend.'

Dr Brown left as suddenly as he had appeared. Mrs Duke held her husband's hand tightly and said, 'You said Dr Brown was in Dundee, Dr Campbell.'

'I understood he was. I'm sorry. I didn't know he'd be back so soon.'

'And Ian starts on the tablets today.'

Steering her husband before her, Mrs Duke bustled out of the room. Campbell returned to the case folder and noted down Dr Duke's pulse and blood pressure, both, as it happened, those of a fit man half his age. His reflections on the uncertainties of his new post were interrupted when Mrs Duke, recalled by an afterthought, put her head round the edge of the door. Campbell looked up.

'I told you there'd been a mistake.'

A few minutes later Dr Brown came back. 'Sorry about that, just breezing in in the middle of things. But thanks for seeing Ian. I'll drop a line to Donald Minto at Moray Place. Better coming from me, and it'll save you the trouble. As it happened, I didn't actually have to go to Dundee. Sorted the whole thing out by phone and had a couple of hours undisturbed in the lab. I should tell people I'm going to Dundee oftener. So thanks.'

'No trouble. Quite interesting.'

'How's that chap in the ward? New stroke.'

'Mr Thompson?'

'Yes, Thompson. James Thompson.'

'Oh. I'm sorry. I should have mentioned it.'

'An extension?'

'Well, I suppose it started as an extension. He went off quite quickly in the early afternoon.'

'How is he now? D'you get him down to Intensive Care?'

'He arrested. And no luck with . . .'

'Tricky one, David.'

'Probably a brainstem infarct. Looked like a cardiac arrest to begin with, so we did our best. But he really wasn't savable.'

'You know who he is?'

'Well, yes. And I saw his wife, and there was a daughter.'

'Yes . . . But you know he's Tom Leslie's brother-in-law?'

'No, I didn't.'

'Tricky one, David.'

'We did our best.'

'I'm sure you did . . . but these things . . . carry over, you know.'

'I'm sorry.'

'Bad time, David, but you were hardly to know.'

Dr Brown hoisted himself up and sat on the edge of the examination couch, a little wheezy. Campbell waited politely for an explanation of the higher political significance of the afternoon's death on the ward. Dr Brown sat silent and thoughtful, then said, 'But we'll see what we can do for Ian Duke. I put him on the higher dose.'

'Oh.'

'Oh yes, I know we normally randomize, but for a colleague . . .' He smiled. 'Even a colleague like Ian Duke. It's very difficult. Very difficult indeed. But he should do well on it.'

'He seemed quite fit. Physically, I mean.'

'And not too bad mentally. Moderate impairment. Certainly eligible. I just went over a few things with him, quickly, then put him on the five-gram dosage.'

Campbell thought about that, and decided to check the study's protocol before embarking on a detailed discussion of the case with Dr Brown.

'What about his work?'

'His work, David?'

'Yes. He seems to be still practising.'

'After his fashion, David, after his fashion. He won't be doing a lot of harm. Jim McVittie and Heather keep pretty close tabs on him.'

'He was . . . a little difficult with Fiona.'

'Always been one for the girls. But under Heather's thumb when it comes down to it.'

'Is he safe? I mean, to practise medicine.'

'Well, if he's not he soon will be . . . As safe as he's ever been, that is. Not one of your Nobel hopefuls, our Ian. Never was.'

'But . . .'

'I shouldn't worry about it, David. If anything, probably doing less harm the way he is.' Dr Brown glanced at his watch. 'I'd better be getting back to the lab. The mashed brains are calling. I'll be up there till seven or so, then I've got a meeting.' He slid from the couch in a way that reminded Campbell of performing sealions, then smiled. 'What did you think of Heather?'

'Mrs Duke?'

'Yes.'

'Seemed very concerned.'

'Oh, yes. I don't think there's much risk of Ian being allowed to forget to take his big yellow tablets. Did you ring Tom Leslie, David?'

'No, I didn't know . . .'

'I'd better ring him now. Peacefully?'

'You could say that, sir. And fairly quickly.'

'Grand. Thanks, David. I'll maybe leave it to this evening. Tom's a busy chap.'

'The wife seemed to take it fairly well. At first, anyway.'

'That's something . . . Thanks, David. It's a great help to have you here.'

'Thank you.'

Campbell sat at his desk with the case folder open in front of him. Dr Duke was, or perhaps now was not, Case No. 146 in the Edinburgh Auragen Study. That point would need to be clarified quite soon. If he was, various blood investigations, a further series of psychological tests and a CAT scan of his brain would be required. If he was not, and the fact that his dosage was known disqualified him from the randomized blind trial of greater and lesser doses of the drug, it was not clear how he was to be followed up. Campbell filled in the details requested in the first four or five pages of the folder and left it at that for the afternoon. Dr Brown did not like being disturbed in his laboratory in the afternoons.

At the desk, Fiona had recovered her customary poise. 'Sorry about screaming.'

'Sorry he bothered you. I'd no idea he was as bad as that.'

'It wasn't the flashing. Unimpressive as these things go. It was the ghastly leer.'

'Oh.'

'Really close. And breath like a bear's bum.'

'Yes. A bit.'

'I felt sorry for his wife.'

' "It doesn't mean he doesn't like you." ' Campbell had not quite got Mrs Duke's accent, but could work on it.

Fiona laughed. 'As if it happened all the time. Yes. That and his breath. When do you want him back for space invaders and all that?'

Patients in the Auragen study took a number of tests, including one called VDU Progressive Matrices, which was done on a thing like space invaders in a pub.

'Not sure. I don't know if he's really in the study now or not.'

'I saw Bobby whisking them off upstairs.'

'Does that happen a lot?'

'Once or twice. More often recently.'

'What happens about their records?'

'I think Bobby keeps them.'

'Oh. I thought Dr Frank kept the records.'

'Yes. Normally. But the notes on Bobby's specials stay with him.'

'I see. Is Dr Frank around?'

'Don't think so. Have you looked in the terminal room?'

'No.'

'Sometimes worth a try in the afternoons.'

'Thanks.'

Campbell, who had now looked for Dr Robin Frank on three successive afternoons, was sceptical. Again Dr Frank was not to be found. He went back to his office and sat for a time with a large book, reading about something called erythromelalgia, which turned out to be a harmless disorder of the circulation in the fingertips, a curiosity with no known cause or significance, exactly the sort of thing that tended to come up in the short cases in membership exams.

Next morning Campbell arrived promptly at ten o'clock for Dr Brown's ward round. There was no one else about, so he waited in the doctors' room, passing the time with a book of lists of causes of things that came up in membership. At ten past ten, when he was floundering among the twenty less common causes of a high blood calcium, the house officer, Jo Phillips, came in.

She was small, dark and lively, and somehow irreverent and efficient at the same time. She waved an X-ray report towards Campbell and threw a large envelope of films down on the desk.

'You were wrong about Mr Puckering's stomach. So was Barry.'

'Was he?'

'I was right. An antral ulcer. But it's not going to my head.'

'Good.

'Who's Tom Leslie?'

'Old-fashioned general physician. Works here mainly but has some beds at the Southern.'

'Is he important?'

'Fairly. Depends what for.'

'Strokes.'

'I don't think so.'

'Dr Brown came in yesterday afternoon and asked if he'd been to see Mr Thompson. I didn't know about it. I mean I didn't know we'd asked for a consultation.'

'I don't think we had. He's a relative. Brother-in-law or something.'

The house officer smiled.

To Campbell, who had graduated locally, Dr Leslie was senior rather than brilliant, a moderately popular chief, a power of middle weight in the great teaching hospital game, and very much the sort of chap the late Mr Thompson, an advocate, would have had as a brother-in-law. The house officer, being new to Edinburgh, could not, for all her merits, be expected to know things like that. Campbell explained a little. 'Nice old boy. I was on his clinic in fourth year. Told us stories about miracles with penicillin.'

'Bobby's scared of him.'

'Oh?'

'He said, "Are you sure he hasn't been in, Dr Phillips? Do you know what he looks like?" What does he look like?'

'Big and fat. Wears suits with the trousers practically up to his ears.'

Dr Phillips laughed, and Campbell chided her gently for her insufficient respect. Tom Leslie's trousers, like Henry Creech's biscuits and Professor Botley's accent, were small but revered constants in the slowly changing Edinburgh medical scene. Thought returned to duty. 'How's the subarachnoid chap?'

'He's not going to do. The surgeons came and looked at him again and said as much.'

'Do people know? His family?'

'It's been about ten days now. They've got the idea.'

'And what about the Parky chap? Mr Benson.'

'Being sick on his Parotrim.'

'Oh. Walking better?'

'A bit. And being sick.'

'Don't knock it. It's good stuff. Morning, David. Morning, Jo.' Barry Swift, the senior registrar in neurology, was effectively in charge of the Parotrim study. With perhaps a more precise knowledge of Dr Brown's habits than either Campbell or Dr Phillips, he had arrived fully ten minutes after the ward round had been due to start. 'Parotrim-induced nausea has been reported, but only in elderly patients generally also found to have hiatus hernia with reflux. Even the students know that.'

The house officer pointed out that Mr Benson was only sixty-three. Dr Swift asked her if the research occupational therapist had repeated the plasticine sausage test since the dose had been increased. Dr Phillips reported that Mr Benson had told her that cutting up pink plasticine sausages with a knife and fork made him feel even more sick. Dr Swift insisted that as a test it was both standard and well tolerated and should be repeated regardless.

At a quarter past ten Dr Phillips switched on the kettle for coffee. Dr Swift said 'Great idea!' and rushed out, coming back only moments later with four new coffee mugs, bright green in colour, with 'Parotrim: the Acceptable Answer to Parkinson's' printed all over them. 'The rep brought them in for us yesterday. Lovely, eh?'

While it was true that the set of mugs already available, actually a mixed, chipped and sorry collection, needed to be replaced, Campbell had some reservations about the new ones, but, since they were clean and not chipped, he had his coffee from one anyway.

At half past ten Dr Brown's secretary rang from the Neurobiology Unit to the doctors' room on the ward to say that Dr Brown was in the middle of a promising glucose uptake run and accordingly would Dr Swift go round the patients on his behalf. Dr Swift was pleased and perhaps not surprised by this request. He stood up, rubbed his hands and grinned.

'Drink up, Dave. Come on, Jo. Yes, you'd better bring the case notes. And we might as well have the students while we're at it. D'you mind going along and getting them, Dave? They're in the tutorial room just finishing brain tumours with Dr Temple. He won't mind.'

Dr Temple had already dismissed the students. They seemed to have assumed they were going for coffee now and were only reluctantly persuaded to join the ward round with Dr Swift.

'He's a keen teacher,' Campbell said.

'We know.'

Campbell had been working for just over a week with Dr Swift and some of his little ways were beginning to grate already. In particular his playful flirtations with nurses on the ward were becoming painful to watch. Broadly speaking, the more homely the nurse, the more extravagant his gallantry. Today he was lyrical.

'Morning, petal. Looking lovely this morning. New boyfriend, is it? Lucky him's all I can say. Yes, love, if you could just toddle round the Brown patients it'll make a pleasure out of a chore. Lovely.'

The girl in charge, a third-year student nurse with acne, blushed until her various red spots had practically disappeared, muttered something, went off to the nursing station and came back with the nursing notes.

'Who's first then, love? Oh yes. A sad one.'

In the single cubicle nearest the entrance to the ward a man in his late twenties lay on his side in bed. He was pale and haggard, and did not move when the nurse, the three doctors and the four senior students came in.

'All right, Andrew.' It was more of a statement than a question. The patient's lips moved silently. 'The new tube not bothering you? Excellent.' From a polythene bag hanging on a drip stand and filled with something that looked like a large milk shake, a fine plastic tube ran into the man's right nostril. Dr Swift fingered the tube. 'Magic,' he said. 'Comfy, Andrew? Compared with the old nasogastric tubes this stuff's a dream. And easier for the nurses too, isn't it, petal? Slides down just a treat and needs changing far less often. Fine, Andrew.'

Dr Swift ushered the students out, remarking, while he was still in the cubicle, though with his back to the patient, 'These things have transformed terminal care.'

The next patient was an anxious, middle-aged bus driver with much to be anxious about. He had been in the ward since Tuesday for investigation of a gradually progressive weakness in both arms. He was called William Lewis, and Campbell, in his capacity as second most junior of Dr Brown's team, had gone over his case in some detail. Mr Lewis was married, with two teenage sons. He kept racing pigeons, drank moderately and did not smoke. His arms and hands had been getting weaker over a period of two or three months, and the muscles, Campbell had noticed, had been twitching spontaneously as well as gradually wasting away.

Mr Lewis was sitting at his bedside. Dr Swift loomed over him, smiling his glassy getting-on-with-the-patients smile, from certain angles a vacant grin.

'Morning, William. How are we today? Let's see . . .'

18

Taking the patient's hand in his own, he twisted round towards the students. 'Douglas? James? What have we here then? Thin? Hardly a medical term, Douglas. James . . .? Wasted. Yes. This . . .' he fingered the gaunt spaces on the back of the man's hand '. . . is wasting. Wasting of? Yes. The small muscles of the hand. Or, if you want to sound as if you knew a bit more about it . . . What? Yes. It's wasting of the interosseous muscles, Robert. Good. Now I want you to think about the various possible causes of that and we'll come back to it in a minute. And now I'm going to ask Mr Lewis about his occupation. Very important, is occupation in wasting diseases.'

Mr Lewis, a thoughtful and quite well-read man, listened as though he were not there. 'William,' said Dr Swift. Thus conjured again into existence, Mr Lewis looked up. 'William, what is your job?'

'I drive buses.'

'You drive a bus. Is it a big bus?'

'About forty feet long.'

'And for that you need a lot of strength in your arms, don't you?'

'Well, no. They're all power-steering and automatic . . .'

'Obviously we can't have bus drivers with wasted arms. So we're going to try and find out the cause and, if we can, the treatment for William's interosseous wasting. So. What's the innervation of the hands? Mary.'

The girl student had perhaps, until she had heard her name, been thinking about her lost coffee break.

'Well, Mary, we were just wondering if you'd be able to help us by telling us a little about the innervation of the hands. Not all the details. Just the spinal roots and peripheral nerves. So that we can think precisely about William's interosseous wasting. Neurology is a very precise subject, as you know.'

'Eighth cervical and first thoracic roots. And peripherally via the ulnar and median nerves, the ulnar supplying . . .'

'Thank you, Mary. So that gives us something to think about. Causes of wasting. Now let's look at William's *other* hand.'

19

Campbell switched off. Swift's teaching manner, a combination of omniscience and baby talk, was somehow offensive to all concerned. The students looked sullenly at their feet. Mr Lewis sweated in silence. The nurse shuffled her notes. Dr Phillips was least affected. She looked on with the air of someone taking an exceptionally stupid puppy for a walk and watching it fall about attempting to pee against a lamppost. Dr Swift, three or four years ahead of Campbell in the great chain of being, was famed chiefly for his enthusiasm almost as much for his knowledge, and not at all for his clinical judgement, that mysterious quantity without which, sadly, the other two were not much use. He had been a senior registrar for only a few months, which explained some of it, and was evidently on a permanent great-medical-teachers-of-tomorrow trip.

'. . . wouldn't it, Dave?'

'Sorry, Barry.'

'I was saying to the students here, while you were daydreaming about that lovely creature holding the nursing notes, that while you could expect to get through finals with about seven causes of interosseous wasting, it might be better to know fourteen if you're having a go at membership. We've got as far as the brachial plexus, Dave. Klumpke's. That sort of thing. And we're getting on down towards the peripheral nerve problems. Any suggestions?'

'Trauma. Um . . . carcinomatous neuropathy. Mononeuritis multiplex?'

'Nice one, Dave. You could keep the examiners talking about that all afternoon, I'm sure. I hope they ask you about it on the day. Not long now, is it? And some easy ones from the students. Lead. Of course . . .'

Mr Lewis sat steadfast throughout, while teacher and taught assembled a litany of variously unintelligible diagnostic possibilities for his complaint. Did he know, Campbell wondered, that carcinomatous meant to do with cancer; that syringomyelia, which sounded like something from the herbaceous border, was a lingering and sometimes excruciating way to go; or that the most likely diagnosis, motor neurone disease, was relentlessly progressive and invariably fatal?

Having wrung from his junior colleagues the last exotic footnote pathologies, Swift rubbed his hands and bowed to Mr Lewis. 'A very good morning to you, William. And not to worry. We'll soon have this sorted out for you.'

In the next bed was a man with an unusual form of muscular dystrophy, in for muscle biopsy and electrophysiological studies. After him there was a man who had confided in Campbell that, after three episodes of double vision and staggering, he was sure he had disseminated sclerosis. Dr Swift chatted encouragingly with him, avoiding precision in the matter of diagnosis, instead talking airily of 'a form of neuritis' which should be unlikely to bother the patient ever again. The last patient, the subarachnoid gloomily summarized by the surgeons as 'not going to do', lay in the other single cubicle, his face livid and swollen, his breathing stertorous. They did not linger, as the students had been taught on him before.

The round over, Dr Swift beamed at the nurse. 'Thanks, love. You were wonderful.' The girl blushed again, not so fiercely this time, and went back to the nursing station. 'Some jolly interesting stuff in just now, *n'est ce pas*, David? A bit of everything. Just how I like it.' To her credit, Mary, the medical student, was looking at him as if he were mad.

Campbell left the ward and walked a short way along the main medical corridor to the new glass-walled corridor leading off to the Neurobiology Unit. At its threshold shabby NHS linoleum gave way to tasteful mid-brown fitted carpet. Fiona, typing at the reception desk, looked up as he came in.

'There was a call for you, Dr Campbell. A Mr Baxter from London. He didn't say what about. That's his number. It's not urgent, so I didn't put him through to the ward, but could you ring back.'

'Thanks, Fiona. Is Dr Brown still around?'

'I haven't seen him going out.'

'Thanks.'

Campbell's office was on the ground floor of the new unit, looking north towards the Institute's clock tower: not by any means the best office, but an office none the less, and as a lowly acolyte on soft money he was lucky to have it. Though

21

never sunlit, it was new and bright, small but so far tidy, with a desk, two chairs and a filing cabinet. The circumstances of his predecessor's departure had been such that a variety of her files and possessions still remained. Campbell had it in mind to go through them once and for all, deciding what belonged to the Unit, and by implication to him as her successor there, and what should be parcelled up and sent off to her family. At first he had thought it odd that no one had done this already. Having himself put it off for almost a week, he was now more understanding.

On the first try the London number was engaged, so Campbell continued his reading on unimportant vascular disorders, learning far more than he had ever wanted to know about varicose veins. On the second try the number rang out once, and a male voice, crisp and vaguely south of England, said, 'Omar'.

'Oh. Could I speak to Mr Baxter, please. It's Dr Campbell.'

'Oh, hello, sir. Chief Backstay speaking.'

'Oh. Hello, chief.'

Though Campbell had met Chief Petty Officer Medical Assistant Backstay only briefly, in Hong Kong as it happened, he had no difficulty in placing him: a large, jolly, blond man, who had run the shore base sickbay and had secretly learned Cantonese, to the eventual astonishment and discomfiture of his various locally recruited staff.

'How's Edinburgh?'

'All right, thanks. What are you doing in London?'

'Like I said, sir. O M A R. Office of Medical Appointments (Reserves). Chief Milton-Thompson's old job. How are you placed for August, sir? Bit of sea time?'

'I've actually got a job now, chief.'

'Permanent?'

'Not really. But I'm trying to sit membership.'

'Nice study job, sir. Bit of sea time. *Oleander*. Out of Guz with a bunch of makee-learnee chopper pilots. Get your knees brown . . . No?'

'Thanks, chief, but I'm really trying to get some clinical time in for the exam.'

22

'When is it, sir?'

'September.'

'I might be getting back to you, sir, with something else.'

'I'm surprised none of the regular MOs want *Oleander*, chief.'

'Well, sir, they've all got a wife, a couple of kids and a semi in Gosport now. No sense of adventure. I don't know what the navy's coming to. You sure you don't want *Oleander* for August, sir?'

Campbell said he was, but felt he wasn't. For a year he'd been away from Edinburgh, teaching hospitals and the NHS, messing about in the navy as a reservist MO, and had enjoyed it immensely. Chief Backstay's phone call, his slang and his offer of what sounded like a thoroughly cushy number rekindled a certain inclination, not anything poetic about must go down to the sea again, but a renewed awareness of a world where cheerful phone calls resulted in agreeable voyages with sensible, sociable people, where life ran to wargames, cocktail parties and even occasional blockades, and where medicine was practised as a useful art, not as an absurd religion.

'Well, sir,' said Chief Backstay, 'you can think about it, and you've got our number if you change your mind.'

'Thanks, chief. But I think I'd better say no.'

'Cheers, sir.'

'Cheers.'

Campbell put down the phone, thought again about the ward round, and wondered if he had made a dreadful mistake. He returned to his book and proceeded without enthusiasm from varicose veins to the altogether more formidable Takayasu syndrome, horrible but fortunately rare, in which limbs fell gangrenous from quite young people, usually females. There was no treatment.

Outside, across the lawn, two young females, nurses on their coffee break, sat in the sun, with all their limbs intact. The membership exam was still five weeks away, and Campbell's roughly sketched reading programme allowed for occasional lapses of attention.

He had still not quite come to grips with thrombangiitis

23

obliterans, the next vascular horror, when the door of his office opened suddenly and without any heralding knock. A short man in a loud check suit came in, smiled and held out his hand. Campbell got up but did not shake it. The grin faded only slightly and the man said, 'Mike Forrest. Regional Manager. KM Pharmaceuticals.'

'Hello.'

'Dave, isn't it. And call me Mike. I mean, we'll be working together.'

Campbell had not thought so, but his new job was full of surprises.

'You settling in, Dave?' The man sat down.

'Yes, thanks.'

'Haven't we met before?'

'I don't think so.'

'We have, you know. Last year. No. I tell a lie. Two years ago.'

'Really?'

'You were in GI then. With Rosamund Fyvie.'

Campbell nodded.

'I was talking to Rosamund in May . . . At the Southeast Asia Conference on Gastrointestinal Therapeutics. Singapore. Helluva place, Dave. Ever heard of Bougis Street? Anyway, Rosamund was telling me she loves Fremantle. Really getting into the whole Australian bit. It's Professor Fyvie now, you know.'

'I'd heard.'

'Great girl, Rosamund. Of course, it was her work here that really put Duonol out in front . . .' The man smiled winsomely. 'Another KM winner . . . Dave, I've just had an hour with Bobby and he was telling me all about you. Oh, don't worry, it's all good. He thinks a lot of you, does our Bobby. Lucky to get someone like you at that sort of notice, he said. And you've seen a couple of new patients for the Auragen study, he was saying.'

'Two or three.' Campbell was still unsure as to the status of Dr Duke.

'That's great. That puts the Edinburgh group right out there with threequarters of the patients in the study already.

And you know there's seventy right through the protocol and just taking Auragen on a long-term maintenance basis. You probably won't know much about them, Dave. It was Theresa, poor girl, and Bobby himself that did most of them. From first assessment to, well, cure, I suppose we have to call it, for most of them. You got any more new referrals coming in this week or next, Dave?'

Campbell said he thought there might be one or two.

'I know it's summer and all that, but it'd be a pity if things slowed down now. I know Bobby wants to get the magic two hundred through the books before anyone else does. Gives him something to prod the rest with, if you see what I mean, and in a multicentre trial somebody's got to get the answer in first. So Kristall Morgen expects, so to speak . . .'

Outside, the nurses got up and brushed bits of dry grass from their uniforms.

'As you know, it's just a question of getting the right sort of people referred.'

'Quite.'

'In other words, getting the GPs to think about the kind of patient we're interested in. For their own good, as much as anything. The patients I mean. But the GPs too. I always say I've never met a doctor who wasn't interested in research. It's just a question of asking the right people to help with the right things. Did Bobby tell you about the seminar on Saturday?'

'I don't think so.'

'Well, when I say seminar, I mean a proper evening. A sort of local premiere for the new Auragen film. And dinner, of course.'

Campbell smiled and declined.

'I'm surprised Bobby hasn't mentioned it.'

Campbell regretted that he had a prior engagement.

'The Pelicans. Ambassador Suite. Seven thirty for eight.'

Campbell was quite sure it was impossible. Mr Forrest got up to go. 'Glad you're settling in, Dave. See you again soon.'

He left, and Campbell was alone once more with the disorders of the arterial system. He rattled through syphilitic aortitis, the thoracic inlet syndromes and Raynaud's disease, all vaguely familiar, then, that system dealt with, surveyed in a preliminary way the fifty or so pages of small print devoted to diseases of the respiratory system. Though it was little after twelve o'clock, he had begun to feel like some lunch. So formidable was the respiratory system, however, that it might be a good idea to make a start. As a sort of compromise he set out to read from the nose to the larynx, discovering on the way a new horror, lethal midline granuloma, which started rather like a persistent cold but went on to gradual destruction of the face and eventual death. The larynx would have to wait.

As Campbell passed the front desk Dr Brown came downstairs from the office and laboratory suite which formed the top half of the Neurobiology Unit. He seemed quite pleased to see Campbell and stopped.

'Going for some lunch, David?'

Campbell tried to look as though distracted from some more pressing matter by glancing at his watch, then said, 'Yes . . . yes, I was.' Dr Brown paused and eyed Campbell's white coat, which would have immediately limited their options to the hospital dining room.

'The club, maybe?'

'I don't think I'm a member.'

'I'll sign you in.'

'Thanks.'

Campbell went back to his office to get his jacket. As they left Dr Brown paused by the desk. 'A working lunch, Fiona. Then another run in the afternoon.' Fiona nodded. It took Campbell a moment to realize that what was meant was not a painful and wobbling wheeze round the park, but a further study of glucose uptake in what Dr Brown had referred to already as 'mashed brains'. 'So no afternoon interruptions.' Fiona nodded again and carried on with her typing.

They walked the length of the medical corridor, at that time of day more like a gregarious village street than part of a major teaching hospital. People chatted outside the bank sub-branch and lingered around the queue for the volunteer-run newspaper and confectionery stand. There was a small traffic jam outside cardiology, with two large lunch trolleys, waiting for a lift, blocking the progress of an ECG machine on wheels and a man on a trolley whose face was half hidden by an oxygen mask, but distinctly bluish. They negotiated the narrow space left between the lunch trolleys and the wall, Dr Brown first and with some difficulty, Campbell following and pretending not to notice.

'A wee sharpener before lunch, David?'

Once inside the club they had somehow walked briskly past the dining room and into the bar.

'Oh. Thank you. A half pint, thanks.'

'Grand.' Dr Brown, by his bulk and a certain silent resolution, bypassed two or three gentler people who might have been construed as standing waiting for service at the bar, and came back with a pint and something that might have been a single gin and tonic.

'You've earned the full pint, David. You've survived a week with us in the Neurobiology Unit. Well, near as dammit. I always say if you can get to Friday lunchtime you can finish the week.'

'Thanks.'

'Cheers.' Dr Brown downed a substantial fraction of his drink. 'Here's to your future in neurology.'

Campbell, who saw his present job more in terms of paying the rent and the exam fees and brushing up on the silly sort of medicine beloved of examiners, raised his glass anyway.

'And you're going to have a crack at MRCP too?'

'Well, yes. I got the first part about a year ago.'

'From what I know of you, you'll get through.' Dr Brown twinkled a little over his gin. 'If you've fooled them once you can fool them again.'

'Thanks. I think luck comes into it quite a lot too. It certainly did in part one.'

'Chaps like you don't need good luck to pass. Though I suppose with bad luck you could fail, if you see the distinction. Had bad luck a couple of times myself. Met old Shaky MacKenzie over a difficult bitemporal hemianopia. We couldn't both be right, and he was the examiner. I'd call that bad luck. And the second time was in Glasgow. They showed me a wee woman who talked like a budgie. I thought it was dysphasia. They insisted it was dysarthria with a Glasgow accent. So back to Edinburgh, and third time lucky. But you should get through. Get Barry Swift to go over one or two things with you every time you go round the ward together. Keeps you on your toes. Makes it second nature to just reel off six causes of whatever comes up. How long have you got?'

'Five weeks.'

'I don't think I'm examining this time. But I'm bound to know someone, so at least you don't have to hang around waiting for the official results.'

'Thank you.'

'And remember to read the *BMJ*. The examiners all do. They think that's the same as keeping up with the literature.'

Campbell laughed and spilled a little beer.

'How's the ward? That subarachnoid still hanging on?'

'Not by much. But seems comfortable. And the relatives are fully in the picture.'

'Have we got any empty beds?'

'Not just at the moment. But we should almost certainly have at least one by Monday.'

'I see. There's an old girl I'd like to bring in. Saw her on a sort of courtesy domiciliary visit yesterday. Ravelston Orr's mother-in-law, actually.'

Campbell, who had once worked for the hospital's token great surgeon, had never thought of him as having a mother-in-law. 'Really? What's wrong with her?'

'Between ourselves, David, Auragen deficiency. I think we'll be able to do quite a lot for her. So I'll ring the bold Alester and tell him the good news. A bed on Monday, you think.'

'Well, I'd be very surprised if that chap survived the weekend.'

'I'll ring him this afternoon. So how are you settling into civilian life again? Don't you find us a bit dull after a life on the ocean wave?'

'Oh no. No, it's quite interesting coming back after a year away.'

'Did two years in the army myself. National Service. Wouldn't have missed it for worlds.'

'Did you travel?'

'Malaya. The Emergency, they called it. Mind you, the worst emergency I had to face was the night we ran out of tonic. Another, David?'

'Oh well . . . No, let me . . .'

'Gin and tonic, thanks.'

Campbell had a half pint added to his glass. Dr Brown dispatched his second gin and tonic with style and told Campbell he could take his beer into lunch. With Dr Brown in the lead they headed for the dining room. The bar area was busy, and two or three other little groups of people from the Institute had gathered. Passing them, Dr Brown seemed unduly watchful, more eager to be recognized than the others were to recognize him. When they were out of earshot he said, 'Unusual to see two senior physicians from the Southern over here at lunchtime. Alex Cairnie's up to something. Funny chap, Alex. Angling for the vice-presidency of the college, for what it's worth. And as a rule he can't stand old Charlie Warren, and there they are. So he's definitely up to something.'

Over the menu, Dr Brown recovered his bonhomie. 'I've been allowing myself one good lunch a week these days. Realized it was Friday and I hadn't really had one. So I think I'll have the pepper steak.' Campbell ordered less extravagantly, but still overshot his customary lunch budget by a factor of two or three, assuming, as was prudent, that they would be splitting the cost of the carafe of house red.

Though his steak was marred by the near but inaudible conversation of the suspect group of physicians, Dr Brown blossomed once more when the sweet trolley came round. He chose more or less everything, with cream. Campbell had a fruit salad.

'I don't think I'd have taken on another editorship if I'd really thought about the amount of work that's involved with this one.' Dr Brown was deep in an armchair. A drip of coffee hung from his cup, threatening his tie. 'Actually I'm editor-in-chief. I think I could have done without the ''chief'' bit. Sounds like warpaint and feathers.' The drip fell softly on to a yellow stripe. 'But we've got a couple of assistant editors, one technical, one scientific. So . . .' he raised his free hand, palm outwards '. . . me chief. You should write a little paper for us, David. Won't take you long, the rate the Auragen data's coming in. Have you published much so far?'

'No.'

'Nothing from that six months with Rosamund? Faecal vitamins, wasn't it?'

'Nothing worth publishing.'

'Ah. Basic science, see? Nothing in it. Real scientists do it better, and it's the clinical touch that gets things noticed. That's why we called it the *Journal of Clinical and Metabolic Neurology*. Combines the two. We take the lab stuff, but mainly we're after real clinical advances. Ideally, of course, we should all be combining our clinical scientific work with basic science . . . I suppose you're going to say that as director of a Neurobiology Unit it's easy for me to say that. And in a sense it is. But there's no reason why you shouldn't do it too, David. It's all there, and the set-up's just made for quick little studies, neat but publishable, in this or that. You should think about it. Come and see me. Anything publishable from your time with the navy? Interesting case of something or other?'

Campbell reflected on the light and sporadic nature of his recent medical experience: interesting, but not in the *BMJ* sense of the word. 'I doubt it.'

'The question's for ever coming up at interviews for anything from registrar jobs on. Why hasn't this chap, who's good in every other respect, not published a bit more? Gives you that extra edge, David. A hundred and twenty-seven's my latest count, and I'm not easing up. In fact, there's something really big just round the corner.'

The group of physicians emerged from the dining room and passed close by. Dr Brown lowered his voice. 'I don't think it's generally realized . . .' he interrupted himself to grin fawningly at the man Campbell had presumed was Dr Alex Cairnie '. . . just how *good* Auragen is. One or two people round here are in for a bit of a surprise.'

Though it was two o'clock before they left the club, Campbell's sense of guilt was softened slightly by the continuing presence there of many other people also allegedly in full-time employment: members of the broad officer class of the university and the hospital for whom the club catered, people from that station in life of which little is expected on Friday afternoon.

Outside it was sunny and warm and Dr Brown walked more slowly than he had on his way down. Again he took it upon himself to counsel Campbell. 'I'm sorry the job you're in is funded for only another eleven months, David. Not that I wouldn't personally be happy to extend it, but the money just isn't there as yet. So it's really a locum appointment, but a respectable length. And you really should get a couple of papers out of it in that time, if you work at it. Dr Frank and I could easily both give you a hand. And then, assuming you have fairish luck with the membership, you'll be looking for something more substantial. A registrar job, maybe?'

Campbell thought that might be premature and the topic better avoided. 'I've actually been trying to get in touch with Dr Frank. Not the easiest person to find.' Unaware as yet whether Dr Frank was male or female, he avoided the use of a pronoun.

'Brilliant mind,' said Dr Brown. 'Mathematical and computing genius. Unfortunately our Dr Frank doesn't enjoy the best of health.'

'Oh.'

'Gets through the work though. Quite amazingly well.'

'Really?'

'Absolutely no complaints about that.'

The phrasing of that left room for the possibility that Dr Frank, whatever his or her gender, might be the subject of other sorts of complaint. A useful source of information on the point might be found in Fiona. Campbell decided to ask her, if Dr Frank could not be located that afternoon. Dr Brown continued to assist with his career. 'You should have absolutely no trouble throwing together a couple of little papers once the Auragen follow-ups start to come through in bigger numbers. And as far as jobs go, we should soon find you something. It's certainly a growing field.'

'Neurology?'

'I was thinking more of what you're doing. Drug evaluation.

If you like that sort of thing. The drug companies are crying out for people they can trust. Couple of years of that then back to the NHS ladder. Or maybe the academic side. A junior lecturer post. Might even be something locally.'

They waited at a traffic light then crossed the road. A grubby, sunburned man, withdrawing or repelled from the entrance to a pub, veered uncertainly across their path. He gave Dr Brown a shaky thumbs-up and said, 'You an' me's a' right, Jimmy.' Dr Brown smiled and nodded.

'That's another thing we ought to be looking at. Auragen in the management of alcohol-related mental impairment. No reason why it shouldn't work for that as well.'

Campbell sensed a troublesome and unrewarding notion, of the sort casually tossed by the directors of multicentre trials to their more precariously funded minions, and asked politely, 'How was it that you came to be interested in the dementias, Dr Brown?'

Dr Brown's pace slowed and he became suddenly more serious. 'Because dementia – Alzheimer type, the common one – is such a terrible disease. I don't know if you've ever seen anyone you know, anyone you're close to, going down with it. That's what they do. They go down.' He turned to face Campbell. 'Someone you know becomes someone you don't know. And then ends up not knowing you. Not even recognizing you. It's a terrible, terrible thing. I've watched someone with it. And kept thinking surely something will turn up before it's too late. Something that'll do for dementia what we can do for myxoedema, or Parkinson's maybe. All sorts of things have been tried. You know that. Some of them have even looked as if they were going to work. But there's been nothing yet that you could hand to the patient and say, "That's what you take. That'll make you better." But over the last ten years the biochemistry's slowly getting sorted out. Enough for us to know what to look for. And I think we've found it.'

They had stopped. The drunk had followed them and stood listening. 'Right enough,' he said. 'Fix the bastards.'

Dr Brown smiled at him again. 'Come on, David. Back to the treadmill. I see from Fiona's book you've got a couple

32

more reviews this afternoon. And I must be getting back to the lab.'

'Right enough,' said the drunk again, watching with befuddled respect. 'Fix the bastards.'

By the time they got back to the Institute Campbell was beginning to feel hot and uncomfortable too. The majority of the people they passed in the hospital had not spent a long lunch hour in the club. A nursing sister from a ward where he had once worked gave Campbell a small, tight-lipped smile, as though she had always suspected he would take to drink, but it had all happened much sooner than she had thought. After a very long walk along the main medical corridor they reached the turn-off for the Neurobiology Unit. Dr Brown paused before going upstairs.

'Saturday, David.'

'Saturday?'

'We're the home team, David.'

'Oh?'

'So we've got to go.'

He climbed a few steps and smiled down at Campbell. 'I think you'll quite enjoy it once you get there.'

'Has Dr Jankowska moved on?'

Campbell hesitated. Though in a sense she had, it was unlikely that the rather steely-eyed lady opposite would accept a bland or unelaborated answer.

'Unfortunately, Dr Jankowska's no longer with us.'

'Moved on?'

'No.'

'Dead?'

'I'm afraid so.'

'How awful. And I'd been so looking forward to our little chat together. Was it sudden?'

'Very. A road traffic accident.'

'How awful. Such a bright girl . . . And that was an awfully good picture of her in the *Scotsman*. About a month ago. Just after the last time I saw her. In fact, I thought of dropping her a note about it. What a dreadful pity. And who are you?'

33

'Dr Campbell. I've taken over. Doing the sort of things Dr Jankowska . . .'

'But she was brilliant. I was awfully impressed with her myself. And the *Scotsman* rather confirmed it. What a dreadful waste and pity.'

'Yes. It was.'

'I've known a lot of bright girls in my time. Through school naturally. And one gets used to them. But she really was one of the brightest girls I've met.'

'You're a teacher?'

'French and German. Was a teacher, really. Though I still do a bit of coaching. One doesn't meet the brightest girls that way, unfortunately. When was it? When was Dr Jankowska killed?'

'About three weeks ago.'

'Just after the article?'

'Yes.'

Campbell glanced at the record sheet. Miss Stella Tyrrel was sixty-seven. She was lean, even stringy, and wore a small brown hat. As she had just confirmed, Campbell's first guess at her occupation would have been correct. She would always be a teacher.

'And what's to become of her research?'

'It'll go on. It was very much a team effort.'

'The death of a young person is always shocking. My friends have begun to die, and some of my girls, as one would expect. But a brilliant youngster, in medicine of all things. However. *Revenons aux moutons.*'

'Sorry?'

'We're here to test my memory,' said Miss Tyrrel. 'I've just done the matrices and my score's improving. What shall we do first? Paired words or random numbers?'

Campbell started with the paired words and read out slowly 'Roast, silver. Seven, vacant. Accent, nail. Orange, simple.'

Miss Tyrrel eyed him as though he were the one being tested, then closed her eyes as he repeated the words, slowly and clearly.

'Now, I'll say a word and you give me the one paired with it. Simple?'

34

'Orange.'

'Roast?'

'Silver.'

'Vacant?'

'Seven.'

'Accent?'

'Nail.'

'Very good.'

They did four more of the tests. Miss Tyrrel's recall remained perfect. Her speed and precision made Campbell feel like an unfit tennis player losing game after game. 'Your memory's very good,' he said.

The design of the study was such that Campbell did not, while testing follow-up patients, have access to their previous records. He was expected simply to write the score achieved in the test, in this case twenty out of a possible twenty, on a single sheet bearing only the patient's name, age, case number and number of follow-up appointment.

He went on to test Miss Tyrrel's recall of six-digit numbers at gradually increasing intervals. Again she scored high, making errors only when the time interval was quite long and her concentration began to lapse.

'That's still very good,' said Campbell, noting the scores in the appropriate boxes. 'How bad was your memory before?'

'Not as good as it is now.'

'But how bad?'

'I'd meet old girls I knew perfectly well and be quite unable to remember their names.'

He decided against asking about her scores on previous testings. It might sound odd and elicit a teacherish put-down. He still hoped to track down Dr Frank and find out about the records system for himself.

'And are you having any difficulties about taking the tablets?'

'You mean about remembering to take them? Not in the least.'

'I really meant do they agree with you. No problems?'

'I don't think so. I'm very methodical and take them at the same times every day.'

'And they don't disagree with you?'

'Not in the least. In fact, I've felt much better since I began to take them. It's all very straightforward.'

'Well, thank you for coming up, Miss Tyrrel.'

'Thank you, Dr Campbell. I was *so* sorry to hear about Dr Jankowska. Normally we'd chat for anything up to half an hour.'

Campbell stood up as she left, with a vague feeling that he might have been kept in after school if he hadn't.

'Everyone seems to think I'm an expert on Dr Frank,' said Fiona. 'I'm not.'

'Sorry.'

'Have you tried the terminal room?'

'The door was locked and there was no reply.'

'Is it about follow-up assessments?'

'Yes.'

'Just stick them through the letter box.'

'Oh. Right. There's another follow-up this afternoon.'

'Mr Mitchell. Not due till three o'clock.'

'Thanks, Fiona.'

Campbell went back along to the terminal room and pushed the sheet with Miss Tyrrel's latest assessment through the letter box, an unusual feature, he thought, on an internal door. Then he returned to his office and read about a series of interesting industrial lung diseases, mushroom-worker's lung, distillery-worker's lung, paprika-splitter's lung and the like, becoming so engrossed that he did not look at his watch again until ten past three.

He hurried back to reception, hoping that Mr Mitchell would prove to be less formidable than Miss Tyrrel, but found that there was no one waiting. Without missing a beat in her typing, Fiona said, 'I'll ring you in your office when he turns up.' Campbell returned to industrial chest diseases.

At half past three he got bored and went back to reception.

'I said I'd ring you when he turned up.' This time Fiona didn't even look round. 'It's Friday afternoon and it's a nice day.'

Again Campbell returned to his office, eventually to begin a half-hearted sort-out of the relics of the Jankowska era, but that proved too exacting a task for late on a sunny Friday afternoon, so he left quietly at four. After all, he was now expected to work for most of Saturday evening too.

'That's not true. It was a proper coronary with seven days in intensive care, a pacemaker and no more of this jogging nonsense.'

'I still think they rust.'

'But even before the results came through we'd decided against putting any pressure on her about university. And she enjoys horses so much.'

'As far as I know, he never smoked in his life.'

'Automatic or manual?'

'Unfortunately nobody got ill, but she was a wonderful understudy. So perhaps the theatre.'

'And they've had the most awful trouble with locums . . . Mind you, he did drink a fair bit.'

'Cheers.'

'So it's between the GTI and the GLS. My accountant says the GTI.'

'No, white. But separated and he'd just been in Libya. Coining it, apparently.'

'Yes. The automatic.'

'He's not nearly so creative, so we gave him his own colour TV.'

'Either that or the camels.'

'Really?'

'No, his father had a stroke. But quite young. Died.'

'Sounds as if they'd have been better off with a good Pakistani. The patients don't mind them these days.'

'Well, up to a point. Got both O-levels first shot.'

'Torque. That's the difference.'

'Some of these days he'll be caught at it.'

'I'm pretty sure they're the Lomond Hills.'

'I can't remember the name of the drug, but it was a helluva good dinner.'

'He's on this new stuff, but Heather's frantic. They're over there.'

'They don't have to be near Loch Lomond.'

'If it works for him, it'll work for anybody.'

'I think they strike them off.'

'Maybe I *was* thinking of Ben Lomond.'

To the northwest, over the golf course, the firth and the hills beyond it, a long sunset had begun. In the middle distance a lone golfer receded down the fairway. Swallows darted and swooped on insects invisible above the croquet lawn and the rose garden. Doves murmured among the chimneypots. On the terrace the various guests of Kristall Morgen Pharmaceuticals (UK) Ltd relaxed with drinks.

'Glad you made it, Dave. Thought you might change your mind.'

'Oh. Hello.'

'How's your glass?'

Campbell had drunk a large gin and tonic more quickly than he had intended. With a jerk of his head and a brief indrawn whistling noise Mr Forrest summoned a waiter. 'Another double for the doctor, chief.' The waiter went off with an air of one not usually treated in this way. Mr Forrest looked pleased with himself. 'Pretty good turnout, innit, Dave? I mean, with lots of people on their holidays. Seventy-two point three four per cent of invitees.'

Campbell wondered if the representative of Kristall Morgen had just acquired a pocket calculator. 'GPs mainly, I gather.'

'That's right. They're the ones we get the referrals from. Costs the earth, this place, but they come when you ask them to it. Ah. Thanks, Jimmy. Just what the doctor ordered, eh? There you are, Dave. Get into that and then I'll introduce you to Marguerite.'

'Thanks.' The golfer was now stooped on a green.

'D'you play golf yourself, Dave?'

'No. No, I don't.'

'Too busy? Well, maybe when you get a bit of promotion . . . Come over here and meet Marguerite.'

Marguerite, whose surname had not been mentioned, was

38

in her late forties and tall, and wore a safe dull dress and sensible flat-heeled lady-doctor shoes. Conversation was general and a little confused, as an impression had been acquired that Campbell was a trainee in general practice.

'I must say I never seem to miss all this vocational training you're getting now. I mean, you pick up the things you need as you go along. And if you can't talk to people you shouldn't be doing medicine. And you pick up quite a lot of the modern stuff at things like this. Are you at the stage of looking for somewhere, or is a partner retiring?'

'Whereabouts are you?'

'Easterdykes. I'm with Harriet McCann. We don't have a trainee. I really can't think why.'

Campbell had a fair idea. As a casualty officer he had dealt with muddle, trouble and occasional disaster from the Maxwell and McCann practice, though at the time he had charitably assumed both partners were in their late seventies.

'We share our on-call with the Brodie, Ellis and Adams practice. You might know their trainee, a wee girl with an MGB.'

'I'm not actually in general practice,' said Campbell. 'I've just joined the Neurobiology Unit.'

'Oh. I thought . . . Well, never mind. Yes, you've got two or three of ours. Willy Robson. And wee Mrs Shanks. No, she died. And that woman who had to get the fire brigade when she forgot about her chips. She's doing all right now. And you want some more? Maybe Harriet's got some. I'll see her about it tomorrow. No. Tomorrow's Sunday. But I'll mention it to her.'

'Thank you.'

'Who's head of that department now?'

'Well, Dr Brown's head of the Neurobiology Unit.'

'No. I meant the department of neurology. The professor.'

'Professor Aithie's retired, as you probably know. But there's been no new appointment yet.'

'My husband was talking about it. But maybe I got it wrong. I thought they'd appointed somebody. No. He said they were about to advertise it. He's in neurosurgery. You probably know him. John Maxwell.'

'Oh. Yes. He taught us in fourth year . . . Are you both Edinburgh graduates?'

'Yes. That's right.'

It was said, Campbell had always thought untruthfully, that a former dean of admissions, an eccentric and a misogynist who deeply disapproved of women in medicine, had recruited, for five successive years and in order to provide substance for his views, the stupidest girls he could find. Campbell did a little calculation based on the approximate dates and Dr Maxwell's apparent age.

'We graduated in nineteen forty-nine,' she said helpfully.

Slanting sunshine, golden under a bluish-grey reef of clouds, lit the string of coastal towns opposite. A small tanker, toy-coloured orange and white, crawled west over dark water. The swallows darted lower over the terrace.

'It's awfully nice out here,' said Dr Maxwell. 'We tried to buy a wee cottage just along the coast. You've no *idea* what they wanted for it. And that was when we still had three children at good schools.'

Campbell murmured sympathetically. Her glass was empty. He offered to go and fill it. 'Was that a dry sherry?'

'Sort of medium dry. Just a small one.'

Approached with only ordinary tact, the waiter at the little open-air bar was cheerful and helpful. As Campbell was leaving, Dr Brown, with an empty glass in each hand, passed him. 'Circulate a bit, David. But for God's sake look after Marguerite Maxwell too.' Campbell nodded, and resolved to do his best on both conflicting counts.

Dr Maxwell was talking animatedly with another large lady in a dull dress and flat heels, and as Campbell approached held out her hand for her glass without looking round. Campbell decided to circulate and found Dr Minto at a loose end. As one who had once briefly taught him, Dr Minto was more familiar to Campbell than vice versa. Campbell introduced himself and Dr Minto made a polite gesture of remembering him. In order to have something to talk about other than how little they knew of each other, Campbell raised the topic of the patient Dr Minto had referred, the demented Dr Duke.

'Yes, Bobby rang me. Sounded quite optimistic. Awfully encouraging to see some progress being made with the dementias. And he seemed to be saying that the higher dosage really was a big advance. Asked me just to keep an eye on things with Ian. I suppose he meant side-effects.'

'Side-effects?' Mr Forrest appeared at Dr Minto's elbow. 'You can't be talking about Auragen. Safe as houses and, what's more, the patients love it. How are we . . . Donald?' Dr Minto raised an eyebrow. 'Young Dave here isn't spreading alarm and despondency, I hope.'

'Oh, come on, Mr Forrest.' Dr Minto set rather a ponderous example on forms of address. 'You chaps are for ever telling us your latest poison's safe as houses.'

Forrest raised his glass. 'If Kristall Morgen had thought up some stuff called whisky and thought about selling it, they wouldn't. They simply wouldn't. Headaches. Gastritis. Cirrhosis. Hangovers. And the same for that stuff you're drinking, Dr Minto.' The point had evidently been taken. 'Some firms might ignore all that and sell it anyway. But not Kristall Morgen. Very ethical, is Kristall Morgen. Everything's checked, double checked, then checked again. So they don't get things wrong. We don't call it Christalmighty among ourselves for nothing. Auragen's a Kristall Morgen product. It works and it's safe, and that's why we want you to get your patients onto it, Dr Minto.'

A consultant at the Institute, with a prosperous New Town private practice, Donald Minto was not famed for cleverness. Sensible and a bit old-fashioned, he was unmoved by the rep's enthusiasm. 'Come on, Mr Forrest, you know as well as I do that if a drug's got effects, it's got side-effects. No exceptions.'

'I agree,' said Forrest. '*Until Auragen.*'

Campbell thought of an exception or two to Dr Minto's little rule. Penicillin was one, if you ignored allergies. Then he thought how few others there were. Dr Minto turned to him. 'Now you're probably a bit young, Dr Campbell, to remember some wonderful stuff we were all told about once. It was called Dista-something. Thalidomide.'

'That was the drug that changed the rules,' said Forrest,

41

smiling sympathetically up at Minto. 'And that was years ago. Sure, it was a disaster, but it led straight to the safety we enjoy today.' Campbell wondered if drug reps were specially trained somewhere with stock replies to the standard forms of resistance. 'The world has changed since then,' said Forrest. 'We've got to get it right now. And at Kristall Morgen we do. Gin and tonic?'

'Thank you,' said Dr Minto. Forrest trotted off. 'And you're with Bobby now, um, Cameron? Hm?'

'Yessir.'

'That with the foreign girl?'

'No. She died about a month ago. An R T A.'

'Yes, of course she did. And we really can't afford to lose people like that, can we? Ah, thank you, Mr Forrest. Now I must just catch Ronnie Kirk about one of his patients . . . before we go in. Excuse me.'

'Nice old gent, Donald,' said Forrest as he went. 'But dead wrong on that one. Never mind. Having a few other teaching hospital people around always helps these things along. Touch of class. Does private too, doesn't he?'

'I gather so.'

A few yards down the terrace Dr Brown appeared to be sharing a joke with Dr and Mrs Duke. Mrs Duke noticed Campbell looking round, and averted her eyes and smiled fixedly at Dr Brown. Campbell recalled her concern about what she had called 'avoiding professional embarrassment'. If they had truly been concerned, they might have declined this particular free dinner. Mrs Duke's voice floated over. 'Of course, we're delighted Dr Hanrahan's . . . well, still alive. And fortunately the clause of the practice agreement dealing with who pays for his sick leave is absolutely watertight.'

'Absolutely watertight.'

Further along the terrace an ungainly girl from Campbell's year, a trainee now in a plush suburban practice, was shrieking delightedly as a much older and drunker man illustrated some point in an anecdote by putting one finger on the end of his nose and crossing his eyes. The two tall women were giggling together and the discussion of cars, between two dapper male practitioners, had broadened to include engine-revving and tyre-squealing noises. Forrest turned to Campbell. 'They're just about drunk enough, Dave. Let's get them in for the film while they can all still see.'

'Papa Victor Kilo to Manston. Five minutes to finals. Over.' In a dimly lit airliner cockpit one of the two younger members of the flight crew glanced anxiously at the other, coughed and said, 'But, *Kapitän*, where is this Manston?' The senior pilot, still staring into the darkness ahead, said, 'Ach, yes. Did I say Manston? Mannheim. Mannheim. This is Papa Victor Kilo to Mannheim, I say again Mannheim. Five minutes to finals. Over.' By the glow of the instrument panels the two younger men looked first at their captain, then at each other, then again at the captain, then shook their heads in frowning Nordic gloom.

The next scene showed the captain, still in uniform, sitting in a bright modern corridor outside a door labelled 'Chief Doctor'. A trim middle-aged man in a white coat, with a stethoscope round his neck, appeared and said, '*Kapitän* Angström, come in please.' The door closed and a meticulously enunciated baritone voice-over said, '*Kapitän* Angström is smitten with the disease of Alzheimer . . . Fortunately, it can now be treated.' The corridor scene faded and the title appeared, in pulsating letters glowing in red and gold. 'Auragen,' it proclaimed, 'the Answer.'

'Every year thousands of men and women like the *Kapitän* Angström are so smitten by the disease of Alzheimer. Formerly there was no hope. Now there is hope. But let us look first at what would be happening to the *Kapitän* until now . . .'

In bewildering succession, the captain, or a series of increasingly aged actors vaguely resembling him, was stripped, examined, X-rayed and portrayed sitting miserably while three doctors stood over him simultaneously shaking their heads slowly in despair. For a few seconds he sat at home looking vacantly out of the window, then he was led shuffling to a car by his tearful wife, to be driven up a twisting road to a bleak mountain sanatorium. As the wife drove back down alone, sobbing at the wheel of her Volvo, the captain was taken to a ward of grinning and grimacing dements, stripped and dressed in a shroudlike white gown and thrust into a restraining chair by two bulky aides.

'Until now,' said the voice, 'the disease of Alzheimer is the relentless progress of dementia. The neuronal connections of the cortex of the cerebrum become atrophied, with withering and dying . . .' For those members of the audience whose terminology might be getting rusty, a helpful animated drawing of brain cells flashed and sparkled, brightly at first, then dimly and more slowly, then, presumably with withering and dying, the cells shrank to darkness. A scientist appeared, standing in a vast gleaming laboratory. The voice spoke again. 'Years of patient research by Kristall Morgen biochemists, physiologists, pharmacologists and clinical experimentalists have now borne the fruit.' The animated brain cells sprouted, stretched and began to twinkle once more. 'Auragen,' said the voice, 'the Answer.'

Campbell was sitting at the back of the room near the projector, and had to strain to listen above its whirr. In front of him the audience of thirty or so was variously attentive or beginning to doze off. Several million poundsworth of scientific equipment gleamed and flickered. 'The Kristall Morgen researchers began by determining the molecular structure of the acetophenyl ketolase molecule, a key enzyme in the maintenance of neuronal metabolism . . .' An impressive object, a sprawling modern artwork constructed of coloured ping-pong balls, loomed into focus.

'Studies on this molecule and its various dephosphorylated substrates led the way to what Dr Boris Engelman, head of the Kristall Morgen Cerebral Metabolism Research Laboratories at Hamburg, has called mankind's greatest ever leap in neurochemical therapeutics . . .' Dr Engelman, small and glossy, smiled severely at the camera and said, 'We begin wiz phosphorylated acetoglutyl. So.'

In the five or six rows in front of Campbell heads were dropping forward one by one. To the left, someone, possibly Dr Duke, had begun to snore, at first fitfully but soon settling

44

to a smooth andante. On the screen, Dr Engelman wielded models of increasing complexity, clicking them together and snapping them apart like an appliance salesman demonstrating a series of irresistible extras.

'And so . . .' He beamed, locking a final armful onto a model now much bigger than himself. 'And at last, we have the answer. Auragen.' Reaching into the pocket of his white coat he produced a handful of large yellow tablets. Again the flaming caption in red and gold filled the screen. 'Auragen: the Answer.' A few bars from an electronic transformation of the end of Beethoven's Ninth rang out and the caption faded. Someone in the audience hiccoughed loudly.

On the screen *Kapitän* Angström reappeared, once more in uniform, bounding across the tarmac to a waiting airliner. At the foot of its steps he paused, glanced at his watch, took a large yellow tablet and bounded on up into the cockpit. 'Auragen,' said the voice over, 'the Answer.' The plane took off and was seen high above the clouds, then landing somewhere in the tropics. Angström and his crew, now accompanied by three Nordic beauties in uniform, walked happily together across to the terminal, and were last seen on an idyllic beach, sunbathing. With a stewardess rubbing suntan lotion into his shoulders, Angström in close-up took another of his large yellow tablets and winked. 'Auragen: the Answer' appeared for a last time in letters of fire and faded to the strains of more electronic Beethoven. Forrest got up, switched off the projector, walked round to the front of the audience and said, 'Thank you, ladies and gentlemen. That almost concludes the educational section of this evening's meeting. If I can interest you in the further adventures of *Kapitän* Angström and his crew, there's another short film that will be shown here for . . . those who wish to stay a little while after dinner and before the drive home. And I think Dr Brown wants just a brief word with you . . . Bobby.'

Dr Brown waddled round the end of the front row and stood framed by the screen and smiling. 'Thanks, Mike. And I must also thank every one of you for giving up a valuable evening of your off-duty, particularly in the middle of a weekend, to come away out here to this little symposium. On behalf of Kristall Morgen, I'd like to thank you also for your continuing cooperation in what is turning out to be, I think we can now say, a truly landmark drug evaluation in the field of the dementias. I'm not going to keep you from what I believe will be an excellent dinner, but I would be doing less than my duty to our sponsors for this evening if I omitted to remind you that the Edinburgh Auragen Study is still recruiting new patients. You know the kind of people, with mild to moderate dementia and good general health. You should also know, and I think either Mike or myself will have mentioned this to most of you individually, that the Edinburgh study has now accumulated some very significant experience of Auragen, particularly in the new higher dosages.

'As you also know, the Edinburgh study is part of a multi-centre trial, with other studies going on in Tijuana, Aix-en-Provence, Bilbao, Bucharest and Puerto Rico. But in terms of sheer numbers in the study and data collected on the effects of medium-term treatment, Edinburgh is . . . well, there's no harm in saying it . . . far ahead of the rest of the field. And that's largely, even exclusively, thanks to your wholehearted support and cooperation.'

A certain restiveness in the audience made itself known by the shuffling of feet and the creaking of chairs. Dr Brown began to talk more quickly. 'I really mustn't keep you from your dinner a minute longer. And may I particularly recommend the hock that comes with the seafood starter . . . but please keep referring patients. Despite, um, a sad loss from our staff at the Neurobiology Unit, and the growing task of keeping track of all our follow-ups, we're still very much in the business of looking for new patients, to bring us up to that two hundred we need. And just one final point. Kristall Morgen is particularly interested in the views of general practitioners, and especially of those with extensive experience of the drug. So there are four places reserved for Edinburgh in the symposium on Auragen to be held in the Eastern Mediterranean a little later in the year. That's for those who have had extensive experience of supervising Auragen therapy in general practice. So bear that in mind . . . if you come across a patient who might benefit from referral up to us. Thank

46

you, ladies and gentlemen. Mine host has assured me that his staff are ready when we are. I'm sorry to have taken up so much of your time. And thank you all again for coming along.'

''Ello, Dave. Didn't expect to see you at one of these.'

'Oh. Hello.' Campbell hesitated. The man's voice was familiar, but his face was not, or at least not immediately.

'You joined the club? Doin' GP now?'

'No. I'm with Dr Brown in the Neurobiology Unit.' Campbell decided that the man's face, under its hair, might be familiar after all, and mentally removed the large moustache and a set of whiskers of a kind known in the navy as bugger's grips.

'Forgotten my name, 'aven't you. Bert. Bert Able. You were on the other side of our body.'

'Of course.' The accent, an unimproved Yorkshire, had been one of three such across the dissecting table. Campbell and his more diffident fellow-Scots on the left-hand side of a wizened male cadaver reeking of formalin had been variously amused, cowed and irritated by conversation and behaviour on the right, which had seemed to reflect an ideal of medical studenthood normally seen only in the cinema: a relentlessly comic and ghoulish comradeship. The Yorkshire trio had also given the impression of knowing a great deal, and it had therefore come as a surprise to the port crew, so to speak, when the starboard crew had gone down with all hands in the second professional examination. Two had disappeared for ever and one, Able, had survived only by repeating the year, graduating a year later than Campbell and his erstwhile cadaver-mates.

'I 'ad to repeat the year, you know. All that fooling about first time round.'

'Seems a long time ago.'

'Be about eight or nine years. I'm in practice now, as you would have guessed. On me own, in Lambhill Terrace.'

'How's that working out?'

'Pretty good if you don't mind work. Took the practice over from an old fellow. Muir. Drank.'

47

'I think I saw some of his patients in casualty.'

'Surprised you didn't see 'im too. Eee. Look at that.'

The medical party had most of the tables in the dining room. The remainder were about to be occupied by the group Dr Able had just pointed out to Campbell: a platoon of middle-aged Japanese men all wearing tartan golfing trousers and blazers, and advancing on the remaining tables, breaking into parties of four as though under strict tactical command. 'They must do package tours from Tokyo. Dave, d'you know Mary? And Bill?'

Campbell was introduced to the others just as the waiter came round with the first course, a collage of shrimps, mussels and various roes with a creamy sauce. 'Thanks, lad,' said Dr Able. 'Looks good. And don't be too long with the wine.'

'The wine waiter, he weel be round shortly, sir.'

'Thanks, lad. Well, Mary? How about us goin' to the Eastern Mediterranean, eh? Where do you think 'e meant by that? Corfu? Cyprus, maybe. Anyway, 'ow about it, Mary?'

Mary, young, evidently single and definitely awkward, blushed scarlet and speared a shrimp. Dr Able had changed little with the passage of the years. He looked round for signs of an approaching wine waiter.

Conversation became more general, in the sense that Dr Able talked a lot, Campbell a little, Bill not at all and Mary only when laboriously chaffed or bullied by Dr Able. The wine referred to by Dr Brown turned out to be a hock with 'Bottled exclusively for Kristall Morgen Gmbh' on the label. An elaborate preparation of little pieces of fillet steak followed the fish, and the wine waiter brought two bottles of a claret much better than Campbell was used to. It did not entirely please Dr Able. 'Sharp, as reds go . . . Have to do though. They have trouble with their reds here. And another thing. Last time I came here they had the cheese before the pudding.'

Bill spoke for the first time, to say, 'French, isn't it?' The subsequent discussion was limited by the fact that none of the four had actually eaten very often in France, or at least not in any style.

'I hear Theresa Jankowska's dead,' said Dr Able as the

48

cheese was cleared away. 'Saw it in the *BMJ*. First in our year.'

There had been a brief obituary, in which the word 'promising' had appeared twice. The late Dr Jankowska had started medical school with Campbell and Able, and had spent an extra undergraduate year in one of the honours preclinical science courses, graduating with a first-class degree. After qualifying, she had practised medicine for just over two years. It was said that while some distinction was required for an obituary in the *Lancet*, the *BMJ* asked only that your subscription was up to date.

'Funny woman,' said Dr Able, as though inviting disagreement.

'I don't know much about her.'

Though Campbell now held Dr Jankowska's old job and occupied her former office, which still contained an unsorted collection of her possessions, he really knew very little about her. A lean, rather shrill little blonde girl with sharp features, she had been an unmemorable member of the class below his, had done good teaching hospital house jobs, had returned briefly to one of the preclinical departments, then reappeared as a Kristall Morgen junior research fellow attached to the Kristall Morgen Neurobiology Unit.

'Full of wind and piss,' said Dr Able. Campbell wondered how it was decided who wrote the obituaries in the *BMJ*.

After the cheese came a choice of *crème brûlée* or a rather mannered fresh-fruit salad of nectarine, guava, passion fruit and apricot. Dr Able persuaded the waiter to serve him portions of both, and drank most of the accompanying bottle of Sauternes. Campbell found himself talking more with Bill, as Dr Able worked on Mary's doubts about the second film, about which he talked enthusiastically ('It'll be a real class movie. Authentic locations, like, and tasteful, if you know what I mean. No violence. Just sex'), so that Campbell wondered if he had already attended an educational evening on Auragen.

*　　*　　*

49

Despite being deep in an armchair with coffee, brandy and a cigar to hand, Dr Brown did not appear particularly relaxed. Though it was hard to know how to judge these things, it appeared to Campbell that the evening had gone well. He said so. Dr Brown sucked nervously at his cigar then said, 'Did Marguerite Maxwell mention anything about her husband?'

Campbell said that she had mentioned him only briefly.

'Odd chap,' said Dr Brown. 'Obsessional neurotic. But a lot of influence. What did she say about him?'

Campbell reached for his coffee. 'Just mentioned that he was in neurosurgery.'

'Nothing else?'

'Not really. No. I don't think so. I sort of remember him from fourth year. He talked to us about the surgical management of aneurysms. Small and a bit intense.'

Dr Brown reached for his brandy. 'That's him. Small, but a lot of influence.'

Across the lounge the Japanese were sitting together talking quietly and one at a time, presumably about bunkers and four under pars.

'It's hard to tell which way he'll go.'

'Sorry?'

'Which way he'll go. Assuming he's on the committee.'

Campbell drank his coffee and waited. Dr Brown blew a smudgy smoke ring. 'I couldn't really believe that Aithie would actually go early.'

'Oh.'

'He could easily have gone another year, doing as little as he wanted. That would have helped . . . Plenty of time, in fact, the way things are going now. But with him going early, it really is touch and go.'

'What age was he?'

'Sixty-one. Looked older. He was probably doing the right thing in his own terms. Hasn't had much of a life for years.'

'Really?'

'Angina and hypertension. Spaced out on beta-blockers for his last few months. Still had angina getting to the upstairs ward, which as professor he really didn't have to do. And, of course, his wife really wanted him out. But, even so, he could still have gone on a bit longer. Just to let us get the Auragen results really sorted out.'

'I see.'

'And Jessie . . . Well, I just never knew . . .'

'His wife?'

'Free Presbyterian. Quite irrational about some things. I think she really pushed him to get out. Hard to tell. You don't know J. K. Sinclair, do you?'

'No.'

'Another Free Presbyterian. He's a senior lecturer at Queen's Square just now, and he'd quite like to come back to Edinburgh. As professor.'

'I hadn't realized.'

'And John Maxwell is as likely to be on the committee as anybody . . . A Drambuie with your coffee, David? Sure?'

It was after eleven. Campbell declined. Eventually he and Dr Brown left the lounge to the Japanese and walked along an elegantly alcoved corridor towards the front door. The second film had evidently just ended. A few of the participants in the Auragen seminar lingered in the foyer. Most carried bottles of the recommended hock. Some had already gone to their cars, and Campbell walked to his carefully, as doors were being slammed and engines revved around him. To the left, over a low wall in the rose garden, someone was being sick. Campbell recalled Mr Forrest's remark to the effect that he'd never met a doctor who wasn't interested in research. It was just a question of asking the right people to help with the right things.

PART TWO

'I want a diagnosis for Mr Munro's cough, Dr Campbell. He's one of your short cases. Let's make him a really short case. You can't examine him and you're only allowed one question.'

'Oh. Well . . . Mr Munro, what's your job?'

The patient drew breath to reply, but instead coughed and spluttered and went very red in the face. He was laughing as well as coughing.

'This is a classy exam,' said Dr Bertram. 'He really has got a cough'. The man laughed again, coughed a lot more and took a deep breath. 'I keep a budgerigar shop.'

'Lucky one there, Campbell. So what's he got?'

'Psittacosis?'

'Say it. Don't *ask* me.'

'Psittacosis.'

'Right. Got a lot of sick budgies in. Psittacosis. Now *he's* got it. But lucky, Campbell. Very lucky . . . Why d'you ask him about his job?'

'Just been reading about industrial chest diseases.'

'Is this an industrial chest disease?'

'Not really.'

'Come on, Campbell. It either is or it isn't.'

'It's not. It's an infection.'

'Right. Treatment?'

'Tetracycline.'

'That would do. What's the organism?'

'Can't remember.'

'Fair enough. Might as well be honest and not waste your time. The more you try, the more you win. Thanks, Mr Munro.'

Dr Bertram ushered Campbell across the ward towards another patient but stopped six feet or so from him. 'What do you see?'

The man looked unwell, in a vague, general way that was easier to recognize than to describe, and his head was nodding gently to and fro. 'He doesn't look well. And he's got a tremor.'

'Bit slow for a tremor.'

'Well . . . nodding.'

'Also known as . . .?'

'Titubation.'

'Rate?'

'About seventy or eighty a minute.'

'Right. A bit slow for a tremor. Cause?'

'Vascular.'

'Know what it's called?'

'De somebody. De Musset. De Musset's titubation.'

'Another lucky one. So what's the diagnosis?'

'Valvular heart disease. Aortic valve.'

'Halfway there.'

'Aortic valve incompetence.'

'So why do they nod?'

'High pulse pressure in the carotid arteries.'

'Fair enough. What else are you going to look for? Want to examine him?'

'Hands. Well, fingernails.'

'Good. Looking for?'

'Oh. Pulsation in the nailbed blood flow. Also from high pulse pressure.'

'Morning, Mr Stevenson. Mind if young Campbell here looks at your hands?'

'Not at all,' said the man, holding them out. Campbell took it slowly, to give himself time to remember what it was called.

53

'Stalling, Campbell. You're right. He's got nailbed capillary pulsation. Whose?'

'Quincke's.'

'Brilliant. Now. Anything else? If I asked you to examine the circulation in his legs . . . I won't. But if I did . . .'

'There's sometimes a murmur in the femoral artery.'

'Mr Stevenson hasn't got that. But say he had. What's it called?'

'Durosiez's murmur.'

'Not bad. It's Durosiez's pistol-shot femoral murmur. Never heard one myself, but it's in the books. So he's got aortic valve incompetence. What's the treatment?'

'Surgery.'

'Right. New valve. He gets it on Tuesday. Thanks, Mr Stevenson . . . Now, Campbell, before we run into over-confidence problems, let's just take a look at Mr Harris's eyelids. Mr Harris . . . another of these young chaps to see you.'

Mr Harris had thickened yellow patches on both his lower eyelids: fatty deposits with an odd name like a Scrabble-winning word, beginning with an 'x'. 'Um. Xanthelasma.'

'Well, that's a start. Thank you, Mr Harris. We'll excuse ourselves now and go and discuss the details.' Dr Bertram backed Campbell into a corner. 'OK, smartass, can you tell me about the classification of the underlying disorders?'

From almost anyone but Bertram, the question would have been faintly offensive. Campbell thought about it then said, 'No.'

'Come on. You can do better than that. Bluff a bit. But not too much.'

'They're fatty deposits in the skin. Associated with high levels of circulating fats.'

'Or, as we say down at the Royal College of Physicians . . .'

'Hyperlipidaemia.'

'Not good enough. They're called the hyperbetalipoproteinaemias now. Types one to four. You better read them up. Now, a last short case. Mr Young's voice. That's him over there.'

'Good morning, Mr Young.'

54

'Good morning,' said Mr Young. His voice was high and hoarse.

'Where do you live, Mr Young?'

'Eighteen Easterdykes Farm Terrace.'

Dr Bertram held up his hand. 'Thanks, Mr Young. OK, Campbell . . . A dazzling display of diagnostic acumen please . . . Got it in one?'

'I don't think so.'

'Feeble, Campbell . . .' They withdrew out of earshot of the patient. 'Come on, what's wrong with him?'

'Well, it's sort of hoarse. And high-pitched.'

'Yes, yes. But what's *wrong* with him?'

Campbell glanced back. Mr Young had obvious, deforming arthritis of his hands and feet. 'Arthritis.'

'Come on.'

'Rheumatoid arthritis.'

'So?'

Campbell could think of no connection and said so.

'Remember the larynx? Joints? Yes, it's got wee joints in it. That's why he's hoarse. Now I've told you about them, can you remember what they're called?'

'Crico something.'

'Crico-arytenoid, Campbell. The crico-arytenoid joints. I don't know what you did with the five hundred hours of curricular time you were supposed to have spent learning anatomy. You've failed your short cases.'

'Oh.'

'Yes, failed. Good start though. Lucky, I suppose, then couldn't keep it up. But not a *hopeless* fail, if you see what I mean.'

'Thanks.'

'You've seen a long case?'

'Yes. Mrs James.'

'Fine. Have a coffee and a think about it while I see if young Bill knows any more than you do about how to do short cases.'

'Thanks.'

Campbell withdrew to the doctors' room and made himself a coffee and sorted out his notes on Mrs James, who had osteoarthritis and diabetes and had been admitted on this occasion with a stroke. As a witness she left much to be desired, rambling on about the time when she had one of her turns during the bad weather and the home help had been late because the buses weren't running because the men that put the grit on the roads had been out on strike. Or maybe that was another time. His notes needed quite a lot of pulling together, but made a bit more sense after a coffee and a quick rewrite.

As he was finishing Dr Bertram came in with Bill, who was looking pleased with himself. 'Played a blinder, did young Bill. Couldn't fault him. Word perfect on the hyperbetalipoproteinaemias. Thanks, Bill. Two sugars. And David here will tell us about his long case. David.'

Campbell began. Dr Bertram listened, interrupted, warned, encouraged, enthused and slurped his coffee noisily throughout, because membership coaching at the Southern's medical unit was informal. When Campbell finished his presentation by outlining his proposed management, Dr Bertram interrogated him in the manner of a slightly manic examiner. 'You said upstairs. How many flights? And the daughter, how often does she actually visit? And when you say she understands her diet, did you ask what she actually eats? Answers, Campbell. One at a time.'

And so it went on. In only a few years Ronnie Bertram had been transformed from a sardonic junior hospital doctor to an enthusiastic young consultant who came in on Sunday mornings to help one or two of the junior colleagues along the membership road. He even seemed to be enjoying himself. 'Bill, You've been sitting there listening to young Campbell trying to pull the wool over the examiner's eyes. Comments? Too many negative findings reported from the systematic inquiry? Yes. A bit vague about sensory testing? Definitely. And him working in the Neurobiology Unit. Dearie me. But a moderately organized attempt, with a reasonable summary, which can cover up for a multitude of sins, and a plan that would get through if the rest of the candidates were really abysmal. A scrape pass, maybe. In a bad year. Not enough to pull you through after those short cases, but OK for a first attendance at the Sunday school. Five weeks and a bit of luck should do it.'

'Thank you.'

In turn Campbell listened to Bill, who had seen a much more difficult case: a man with a biggish liver and a very vague story which sounded, as Dr Bertram put it, like something nasty in his belly. At twelve they finished. Campbell and Bertram walked downstairs together. As houseman and registrar they had once worked closely together. Campbell asked how Bertram was enjoying his new post. 'Sounds daft, but I like it because I've always wanted to look after people. You get to do it when you're a houseman and you don't really get a chance to do it again until you're a consultant. In between, you're looking after yourself, or your boss, or your career, or just your next publication.'

It seemed to Campbell that he might be anything from the second to the twentieth recipient of this credo, but that did not make it any less sincere. If anything, it explained a mild chronic cynicism in the prolonged intervening limbo, and offered an explanation for some of his own present dissatisfaction.

'That makes sense.'

'It's great. I'm still on the high. Every morning when I wake up I think, hooray, I've got a proper job again. And another thing. When I was up there, really since from when I was student, I used to wonder if there was life outside the Institute. There is. And it's great. So cheer up, young Campbell, and pass the wee test and the world's your oyster. Got anything fixed for after this job you're in?'

'No.'

'We'll be interviewing for a registrar in about six weeks. You should think about having a shot at it. So it would look good if you scraped through first time.'

'Maybe a bit early. I thought a SHO job . . .'

'Maybe. But think about it. Has Bobby Brown made you an offer?'

'Only very vaguely.'

'Don't touch it, son.'

'Really?'

An elaboration would have been helpful, but they were already in the car park. Bertram twirled his car keys and said something about picking his wife up after church. He got into his car. 'See you next Sunday, Dave. And remember the hyperbetalipoproteinaemias.'

'Thanks.'

'I don't know what they wanted me in here for these tests for. There's nothing wrong with my brain. Mind you, it's about the only thing you could say that about. I may not have a minute's comfort from one week's end to the next, but my brain really is very good for ninety-five. I sometimes wish it wasn't just so alert. I really do. The agony I go through. But that's the way of it. They said something about my memory. Memory? If only I *could* forget. The things I've been through. That wee English girl asked me about my operations, and I told her. Fourteen. Not including a breast abscess that was done in nineteen twenty-seven without an anaesthetic. Fourteen, including a Colles' fracture with complications, a pin and plate for a fracture to my left hip and a Moore's prosthesis to my right. And I've had a vagotomy and pyloroplasty for a duodenal ulcer and my gall bladder out for chronic cholecystitis. And then I've had a laminectomy for a prolapsed intervertebral disc and of course a pelvic-floor repair for the usual thing. And I had an incisional hernia repaired but it came back. And, of course, I've had cataract surgery. Both eyes. And I had a thyroidectomy for Graves' disease. That's just the important ones. And I had a laparotomy for intestinal obstruction due to adhesions and a partial resection of the large bowel for diverticular disease. With complications.'

'You seem to have a very good knowledge of medicine, Mrs Spence.'

'So I should have. I trained as a nurse here and was a ward sister for seven years. My late husband, the late A.J.A. Spence, whom you're too young to remember, was a physician here at the Institute and my daughter qualified from Edinburgh in medicine. And, of course, my son-in-law's a surgeon. *And* I keep with things. I take the *Reader's Digest.'*

'I see.'

'If you could just forget about my memory and do something about my bowels instead, at least you wouldn't be wasting your time quite so much. But I don't expect miracles. Young Donald Beatty is the only doctor I've met who was even remotely interested in them. Mrs Spence, he said, I have to take off my hat to you. Twenty-six feet of diseased bowel like yours would have finished off many a strong man in half the time you've had them. He recommended sherry. Medium dry.'

'I see. When was that?'

'Nineteen forty-nine. And he said he still couldn't promise a cure. He was right, of course, and I've been a martyr to my bowels for fifty years now. And I also have neurasthenic palpitations of the heart, and flatulence, as you'd expect after a cholecystectomy, and my spine is just riddled with arthritis. But there's nothing wrong with my memory.'

Mrs Spence had been admitted to the ward that morning and was now with Campbell in the Neurobiology Unit, being assessed prior to treatment with Auragen. Though he was now less unfamiliar than he had been with the ways of Dr Brown, Campbell was once more uncertain as to whether a patient was in the randomized trial or not. So far, as she had predicted, he had found little wrong with her memory.

'You're too young to have known my late husband, the late Dr A.J.A. Spence, Dr Campbell, but you've probably heard of my son-in-law, Mr Alester Ravelston Orr. He's a surgeon here at the Institute.'

Campbell briefly acknowledged that he had and then tried to explain about the paired-word test. Mrs Spence did not appear to be listening.

'The war unsettled him,' she said. 'A lot of these young men were unsettled by the war.'

'I'll read out the words slowly, in pairs, and then I'll read them again. Then when I mention one of the words I'd like you to say which one it's paired with.'

'He was in Italy for quite a long time. Away from the fighting.'

59

'I'll read out the words, Mrs Spence. Letter, five. Young, house. Past, apple. Out, reward.'

'It was a terribly worrying time for my daughter. I tried to tell her not to worry. We'd all been through that in the war before. Then for a while he stopped writing.'

Campbell read out the words again.

'Then we discovered from a friend of ours that he'd been home on leave and not told us. Well, not *home*. I mean, he'd come back with some floozy from the Nursing Corps . . . We thought he'd died.'

'House.'

'Young. It was terribly upsetting. So naturally we've kept a pretty close eye on him since.'

'Reward.'

'Out. I think I could say I did all a mother could have done.'

'Apple.'

'Past. I stayed with them. Well, Eleanor had never left home. Because of the war. She was in war work here in Edinburgh. So Alester just moved in with us. My late husband quite enjoyed having another medical man about the house to talk to.'

Campbell, who had never thought of Ravelston Orr other than as a capricious, authoritarian and perhaps incipiently senile surgical grandee, was intrigued, but did not feel it would be professional just to give up mental testing and let her go on and on. 'Five.'

'Letter. He sort of settled down then. Well, he spent a lot of time in his laboratory. I suppose that helped him too.'

'Very good.'

'I only did what any mother would have done.'

'Now I'm going to read out some more words.'

'Mind you, there's no saying what he gets up to at those conferences. He goes all over the world. Up to four or five times a year.'

'How many of you were in for it?'

'They don't tell you that, but they interviewed four. Myself, Andy Lockhart, a woman from Glasgow and one of our colleagues from the new commonwealth. Bolton, actually. Chowder-something. They really don't make it any easier for themselves, with those names. A wee brown chap. Came into the waiting room, looked round and said, "So. I am again the token wog." Then he smiled at the girl from Glasgow. "And you, my dear lady, are the token woman. Good afternoon." So, assuming he was right, it was between me and Andy.'

'I don't know much about him.'

'Good school, nice accent and that's about it. Didn't so much come into orthopaedics as get thrown out of general surgery. He was out at Bavelaw on the rotation, as registrar to old Wullie. Good rough cutting job, but too rough for our Andy. Told Wullie he'd done a rectal on an old biddy with weight loss, and that it was normal: Wullie couldn't understand that, because he'd put the whole lot in the bucket a couple of years before that, taking out her rectal carcinoma. So naughty Andy. Making up stories. What you might call a reluctant orthopod now, but at least he doesn't have to pretend he's got to the bottom of things any more . . . They kept him in there for quite a long time though. Chatting about the old school, one must presume. The other two got a token ten minutes each. Ah, thanks, lad. Yes. A pint. Thirsty work, sitting in there answering silly questions of an afternoon.'

Hadden, bright-eyed with drink and success, sat in the corner between Campbell and the house officer. His interview suit was tight across the shoulders. He had undone his top shirt button and loosened his tie, that of a Fellow of the Royal College of Surgeons of Edinburgh. Campbell got up. 'Pint, Graham? And Jo?'

'Yes, thanks.'

'A pint?'

Dr Phillips smiled. Perhaps a quick second pint was normal among lady medical graduates from Manchester. Campbell went over to the bar. When he returned with three more pints of Old Peculier, Hadden was still talking about his interview.

'Then, when everyone's been interviewed, a lady in a twinset takes in a tray of tea. They drink it, read the tealeaves and decide. Then the chairman comes out and tells you.'

61

'What do they actually say?' Dr Phillips wanted details.

'The chap just says your name, like a butler in a film, and you go back in and they offer you the job. The rest just bugger off. Having claimed their travelling expenses, of course.'

'Are you pleased?'

'Ask not what your bank manager can do for you, but what you can do for your bank manager. I expect mine will be quite pleased. Cheers, lad.'

They were in the Wee Man, an odd little one-storeyed survival from a long demolished slum, where Campbell and Hadden had arranged to meet for a drink after the latter's interview. Dr Phillips was there because at tea on the ward that afternoon she had expressed a newcomer's doubts about the beer in Edinburgh, and Campbell had thought it only polite to invite her along. The Old Peculier seemed to be to her liking, in that of the three she was already farthest down the second pint. Campbell and Hadden watched her. She smiled and put down her glass. Campbell asked Hadden what sort of things people wanted to know at interviews.

'Silly things, mainly. The great thing is to pretend not to notice and try to give intelligent answers. The mad scientists ask about research, so you're in favour of it. The general surgeons want to hear that a good grounding in general surgery's the only possible basis for specialization, so you tell them that. And the chairman doesn't want to be late for his golf, so you don't waffle. It's probably all fixed beforehand anyway. Chaps ringing chaps and having a word. Good references help, but if they're really interested they'll have a word. Get the awful truth, with nothing on paper. Anyway, that's it. Offer in writing, acceptance in writing, a month's notice and off to the department of bone-setting. And how about you, lad? A proper job in sight?'

'I don't think so. I'm sort of concentrating on membership.'

'Ah yes. A thousand and one things every boy should know about things he never sees. How's it going?'

'Hard to tell. The more I read, the more I find I don't know.'

'You'll be disappointed.'

'Fail?'

'No. You'll pass. And it'll be a letdown. The Groucho Marx

bit about who wants to join a club that lets *me* in. But they'll let you in.'

Campbell was sceptical. Dr Phillips said, 'You'll pass.' Campbell recalled saying the same thing to other people in similar circumstances in the past and not meaning it. At the next table a man, drinking alone, was talking to himself. He was small and shabby and not visibly troubled: just a man in a pub talking to himself. At the bar a group of younger men in suits were standing talking to each other. There were two barmen: one older, with old-fashioned Brylcreem hair and a narrow tie, the other young, casual in a tee-shirt and New-Testament-length beard. Had that just happened, or had someone taken trouble to ensure that both the pub's original clientele and its new wave of critically aware beer people felt at home?

Hadden, Campbell and Dr Phillips talked and eventually finished their second drinks. The house officer got up and went for her round, perhaps another distinguishing feature of Manchester lady graduates. The older barman looked on as the younger served her. She waited unselfconsciously, even though the man who had been talking to himself had stopped in order to watch what might have been, in former times in the bar, the unusual if not actually indecorous spectacle of a lady buying three pints of beer. As the barman returned with her change she said something, inaudible from the table, which at the same time made the younger barman laugh out loud and caused the older one to avert his eyes. Back at the table, she distributed the glasses with a sure professional hand.

'Cheers, Jo.'

'Cheers. And congratulations again. Does it mean you have to give a whole lot of lectures?'

'I doubt it,' said Hadden. 'It's an academic post, but the only difference from a straight NHS one is that I'm supposed to nail up the old ladies' hips and sort of think about it at the same time. And the odd little learned paper might not go amiss, I suppose. "The influence of professorial vacations on operative mortality: the case for the twenty-week academic year." That sort of thing. And perhaps a little study of the six commonest orthopaedic cock-ups. I'm hoping to get a grant for that one from the National Council for the Care and Rehabilitation of Offenders. But it's really too early to say to what extent academic surgery is going to change my life.'

Campbell asked if the new post carried senior registrar status.

'Affirmative, praise be to Allah. My job uncertainty resumes now at a significantly higher level.' Hadden elaborated, and Campbell reflected on his own very different position. Dr Phillips, whose employment prospects, if any, were unknown and undiscussed, was cheerful and outgoing, without being drunk, and was the object of intermittent attention from the all-male group of beer connoisseurs in suits.

They finished the round and there was a brief awkward moment. Jo got up, saying, 'I'm going for a pee.' The old man at the next table shook his head and started talking to himself again. Campbell, Hadden and Jo adjourned to the malodorous hinder subdivisions of the pub and reconvened in evening sunlight on the pavement outside. Jo offered Campbell a lift back to the Institute. He declined, as he had arranged to go and eat with Hadden. She got into her large, noisy sports car and roared off up the hill.

'What a big car for a little girl,' said Hadden. 'What is it? A Scimitar?'

Campbell had asked on the way down. 'It's a TVR.'

'Goodness me. And she sinks a fair pint. I really don't know what the Institute's coming to.'

They walked west towards the Grassmarket, along a canyon of derelict shops and warehouses, briefly less grim as the setting sun crossed its axis, then through a vast stone bridge that carried another, more salubrious street overhead. Ten years before, when he had just come to Edinburgh, Campbell had been puzzled by an area covering several blocks in which the city's plan was actually three-dimensional, as streets were carried over the dark slums on either side of the Royal Mile. Now, like everyone else, he had got used to it, and felt sorry for tourists with too simple maps, craning upwards or downwards at what they had expected to be an ordinary intersection.

In the Grassmarket they turned right onto one of the steep streets that joined the two levels, then up a dank, lavatorial stone stairway to a curved terrace leading back, above the Grassmarket with its cluttered, crow-stepped, Hans Christian Andersen gables, towards the castle. The Ensign Ewart was full of soldiers from the Tattoo. They walked on. Hadden paused under a theatrical balcony in Ramsay Gardens and struck a pose. 'It is the east, and Juliet is the sun . . . Did you ever meet Juliet? Caroline, actually. Better class of thoracic night sister. Lovely thorax, even by day. Lived up there on the side facing the castle. It was all right. Except for lunchtime naughties. Used to get blown out of bed regularly by the one o'clock gun.'

They proceeded downhill to the New Town, stopping on the way for a gin and tonic in the baroque splendour of the North British Hotel. Hadden grew gloomy at the wider implications of the afternoon's success.

'It's the S R bit, mainly. If they make you one of those, it's a life sentence. After that, being a consultant's only a matter of time. When, not whether.' He finished his drink and crunched the ice and lemon together. 'And where, of course. You know Gavin's in for a job in the back end of Lanarkshire. And the poor bugger hopes he'll get it.'

Gavin Laird was the senior registrar in the general surgical unit where Hadden and Campbell had first worked together. Even two years previously he had been showing some signs of disillusionment with his lot. 'How long's he been an S R?'

'About as long as you can be. He's in his sixth year. Second extension. The poor bugger had to go along and plead with a committee for the privilege of another year of being shat upon by Ravelston Orr, and say thank you when he was given it. Twice. So he's got to get something soon.'

'What's wrong with the Lanarkshire job?'

'More or less everything that's wrong with the N H S, plus everything that's wrong with the arse end of Lanarkshire. So he's had to go across there and grovel like there was no tomorrow, because maybe there won't be. Six years is a long time as an S R. Very few make seven. As with dogs, one year counts as ten, more or less.'

They left the North British and walked along Princes Street, where little clumps of tourists were looking contentedly in the windows of closed shoe shops, then turned a few blocks north to a bar, previously unknown to Campbell, in a distinctly unsmart New Town back street.

The barman seemed to know Hadden. 'Hello, you old bastard,' he said. 'You've just missed Bill MacMillan. It's all fucking orthopods tonight. He was looking miserable too.'

Hadden introduced Campbell. 'Sandy . . . David. Sandy's the proprietor here. And the barman. And the most faithful if not the most diligently paying customer. And he's well known as an ardent pacifist.'

'Pacifist, my arse.' Without looking, the man reached back to a dusty shelf, grasped a large military sword, swung it round his head and banged the hilt twice on the bar counter.

'See what I mean?' said Hadden. 'One of the most militant conscientious objectors ever to serve with the Seaforth Highlanders.'

'You old bastard,' said the barman. 'What are you drinking?' He tested the edge of the sword then laid it down on the bar.

'Drams,' said Hadden, speaking as though he had lost interest in the matter. 'Just drams.'

'We have Glenmorangie. That's a light breakfast whisky as pleasing to the palate as to the eye. And Bladnoch, with its lingering fruity aftertaste betraying its far-off southern origins in Wigtownshire. And Bell's if you just want to get drunk.'

'Bell's,' said Hadden.

It would have been surprising, perhaps even disappointing, if the glasses had been clean. The bar was dark and defiantly unimproved, its only decorations being a Schweppes poster of a lady draped in black, possibly dating from the forties, an enormous Scottish international rugby shirt and a dusty print of the Declaration of Arbroath. The woodwork still carried the matted, cracked varnish of perhaps fifty years ago and the floor covering was worn linoleum. There were no other customers. The barman pushed a water jug towards Campbell, as though what he might do with it were some kind of test, failure in which would lead to a further outburst of swordplay. Campbell added a judicious volume, slightly less than equal to that of the whisky. The tension relaxed a little.

The barman turned to Hadden. 'Still at the Institute?' Hadden nodded over his whisky.

'I've nae time for it.' From under the counter the barman produced a half pint glass of milky tea and sipped it and coughed. 'I went in there just not well. Wind, you know. But I came out with bloody cirrhosis.' He drank more tea. Drops hung from his moustache. 'And they've already got half my stomach. A partial for ulcers.' He put down his tea and pulled his shirt open. Hadden leaned forward and inspected a neat white scar. 'Who did that?'

'The late A. J. Lorimer. Did you know him?'

'I missed him,' said Hadden, 'but I've seen a film of him operating.'

'A fine man,' said the barman. 'He died of drink too.'

Two more customers had come in. One of them was a junior hospital doctor a year or two behind Campbell, a man from somewhere in the north, clever but a little detached from the mainstream of teaching-hospital life, familiar from the Institute and its adjacent pubs. He was tall, with an early middle-age spread, and wore a bracken-coloured tweed jacket with scuffed leather cuffs and elbow patches. His companion, taller and thinner, in a gaberdine with a hint of navy surplus about it, stood silent as he addressed the barman in Gaelic. The reply, also in Gaelic, was probably, from its phrasing and delivery, obscene but not unfriendly. The barman switched to English. 'And Paul. How nice to see you. What'll you have, boys?'

They took malt and fussed over it like serious whisky men. The junior hospital doctor looked round the bar, recognizing Campbell, who in turn remembered his name: Ian MacLean. 'Hello, Ian.'

'Hello, David. Oh. Hello, Graham.' Campbell would not have guessed that Hadden and MacLean would have known each other, except in the sense that in the little world of Edinburgh medicine everyone might know everyone else.

MacLean introduced his companion, the tall, sombre English-man, then said, 'And how's the world treating you, Graham?'

'Could be worse, I suppose,' said Hadden, not sounding at all like a man who had just gained an important promotion. 'Yourself?'

'Och, I'm still in four and five, as an SHO. Silly sort of job, but there's time to read . . . I'm getting ready for a wee go at the first part of the membership, I'm not sure why. So I'm having a night away from the books.'

'The college needs your money,' said Hadden. 'What do you do, Paul?'

'Oh, I'm having a night away from the books too.'

'Membership?'

'No. I'm a publisher.'

'Medical?'

'God no. Just books. General publishing. Cookery books and poets.'

'Poets?'

'Yes. And dreadful novels.'

'Really?' Hadden had regained a little of his customary curiosity. 'Are they meant to be dreadful?'

'No,' said Paul. 'Not at all. One reads hundreds of really dreadful novels, and publishes a few. The least dreadful, one hopes.' He fell silent, a shy man who had said too much.

'You've got your sword out, Sandy,' said MacLean. 'Is it closing time?'

'Oh, no. I'll stay open a wee while yet. It's Thursday, isn't it?' MacLean nodded. The barman said, 'Good, good,' and began to sip his tea again.

Campbell asked MacLean about his job.

'Typical teaching hospital SHO job,' he said quietly and without irony. 'Good thing to have done, but sort of silly while you're doing it. You keep an eye on the house officers and the students. And the registrars, the senior registrars and the consultants keep an eye on you. It's like being on proba-tion. And they're for ever wondering if you'd mind seeing a few patients in the clinic for them. Good experience, that's called. What are you doing yourself?'

'Sort of marking time. In the Neurobiology Unit.'

Dr MacLean put down his glass. 'Is that with that Auragen stuff?'

'Yes.'

'Is it any good?'

Campbell hesitated. 'I think that's what I'm supposed to be finding out.'

Hadden grunted and said, 'It dilates arteries previously rigid with chalk, raises neurones from the dead and gives your average wee dement the brains of Bismarck and the balls of a Munster fusilier.'

'Really, Graham?' said MacLean.

'I'm going to start putting it in my fellow-orthopods' tea. Then young Campbell can come over and casually ask them to subtract seven from a hundred and all that. And, of course, it might bump a few of them off . . . Come on, Campbell. Isn't that drug company paying you enough?'

'Hm?'

'It's your round.'

Before Campbell had opened his mouth the barman had poured two doubles of Bell's.

'Will you have one yourself?'

Before putting the bottle back on the shelf the barman poured an inch into his tea. 'They told me I shouldn't, but there's not a doctor comes in here that doesn't drink himself, so I will.'

Hadden started to talk about Lorimer. 'He trained Lochhead, you know. So Lochhead's got a lot of good Lorimer stories if you get him started. It was all some time ago now, when gasmen were much more dangerous, so speed kept you out of trouble. The college has this clattering old film of one of his famous twenty-two-minute gastrectomies. Blurred and grainy, but you can see him doing it, just sliding in there, like Lochhead himself but cleaner and faster: all feel and touch, not a lot of cutting and hardly any blood. Lovely to watch. Oddly enough, he cut his wrists in the bath.'

The publisher took a couple of deep breaths. 'Really?'

'Usual reasons. Balance of mind and so forth. The boys were very nice about it afterwards, as indeed they always are.' Hadden stared into his whisky.

'You're kind of gloomy tonight, Graham,' said MacLean.

'Promotion,' said Hadden.

'To SR?'

'Lecturer with SR status. A gloomy sort of grade. A year or two or six in the valley of the shadow of a permanent post, itself only a brief sojourn this side of mortality . . .'

'As bad as that?'

'Nearly. But I'm keeping my spirits up. I think of A. J. Lorimer, and take regular baths.'

Later, after an Indian meal, Campbell and Hadden walked up the Mound for a last drink at the club. As they went in Mr Ravelston Orr emerged from the dining room. He seemed to be in good form, and pleased to see two recent members of his junior clinical staff. They were introduced to Mrs Orr, a chilly little woman whose face seemed vaguely familiar. Campbell stood back as Hadden and Ravelston Orr did most of the talking. He was mildly surprised that his old chief had so much as remembered his name, and wondered whether he had chosen to overlook, or simply not noticed, the cumulative effects of their evening's leisure.

Hadden, who had an enviable sudden sobriety for occasions such as this, was asked how his interview had gone.

'Quite well, thank you, sir. In fact they offered me the post. I'll start in the department in October.'

'Oh, well done, Graham. Always pleased to see one's younger colleagues getting on in life.'

'And thank you very much for acting as a referee, sir. I should have rung you earlier about how things went.'

'Not at all, dear boy. In fact we've been out most of the evening. Delighted . . . delighted to hear your news.'

'Have you heard anything from Gavin, sir?'

'Gavin?'

'Mr Laird.'

'Oh. Of course . . . yes. Not yet . . . been out all evening. Yes . . . with Gavin, of course, one always hopes . . . Yes . . . Well, splendid.'

Campbell, having had another look at Mrs Ravelston Orr, sorted out the question of her apparent familiarity. She looked not unlike her mother, now in the ward for assessment, by

70

courtesy of Dr Brown. Perhaps the Ravelston Orrs too had something to celebrate that evening.

When they had gone Hadden said, 'The least we could do is ring the poor bugger.' There was a pay phone in one corner of the entrance hall. Hadden dialled the number from memory and stuffed in a few coins when it answered. 'Hello, Gavin. It's Graham. Oh. Really . . . I'm sorry. Never heard of him. Yes. That's tough. Sounds like the Glasgow mafia again . . . Maybe. Well, you never know. Anything else coming up soon? No. Oh, well . . . No surprises, really . . . Yes. Quite pleased. I don't think Andy was too surprised either. It just goes to show what happens if you neglect your botty-doctoring . . . Yes, a lesson to us all. OK . . . Good-night, Gavin. Thanks.'

Hadden put down the phone. 'Poor old bugger.'

'What'll he do now?'

'Slap in for a few more jobs he won't get. Then it's probably the sands of Araby. Fishing bits of camel and Cadillac out of Arabs from road traffic accidents, and sewing hands back onto suitably affluent malefactors. It wouldn't suit me.'

'Me neither.'

'Certainly not with Glenfiddich at fifty lashes a dram.'

As Campbell walked back home across the park he began to think about the exam again. The barman had demonstrated one or two interesting things, clinical signs of alcohol-related disorders: his volatility and odd behaviour, the dilated, broken capillaries adorning his face and the little red spidery flares on his skin when he had pulled open his shirt. Peptic ulcer was commoner, of course, in alcoholics. His hands too had been quite interesting, with a characteristic tremor, pearly white nails, flushed palms and a contracture pulling his little finger over across to his thumb: all things that were commoner in cirrhotics. An interesting case, thought Campbell to himself, walking under the cherry trees towards the arch of whale jawbones marking the limits of the park: a case, as Hadden might have remarked had he been examining in the membership, of whisky.

*   *   *

71

'Four? Are you sure, Fiona?'

Fiona smiled patiently. 'Yes, four. Three of them from the one GP.'

'Who?'

'A Dr Duke.'

'Dr Duke?'

'Who's Dr Duke?'

'Um. You've . . . met him.'

'Have I?'

'He was a patient here. The chap with breath like a bear's bum, as you put it.'

'Hm,' said Fiona. 'Still at large, is he?'

'Must be, if he's referring patients.'

'It'll be that bossy wee wife of his. She must fancy the Mediterranean symposium.'

'Could be.'

'That, and the thirty pounds a month.'

Campbell, who had now begun to think there were few surprises left in the world of drug evaluation and promotion, was taken aback. 'Thirty a month?'

'Thirty pounds per patient per month,' said Fiona, with an expression evidently meant to convey that she was just the secretary and could not be held responsible for matters of policy. 'There are quite a few of them on upwards of two hundred a month.'

'Really?'

'They're supposed to check for side-effects.'

'And money's no object?'

'I suppose not.'

'Has anything turned up?'

'What?'

'Side-effects.'

'You'd have to ask Dr Brown about that, Dr Campbell.'

'I will.'

'You know he's in Rumania.'

'I didn't.'

'In Bucharest. The mad lady neurologist has been pestering him for weeks. He only decided to go yesterday . . .

72

Did you know that two of your patients are here already, Dr Campbell?'

'Thanks, Fiona.'

By lunchtime Campbell had decided that four new assessments were too many for one morning, and wondered if the sudden access of referrals had resulted from the evening spent at the Pelicans and might be expected to continue. Only one of the patients, however, had anything significant in the way of mental impairment. A placid old widow, almost blind but not unduly troubled about it, she had few complaints. Her daughters visited her frequently, her home help was 'a nice wee girl' and if she wanted to know what day it was she listened to the news on the wireless in the morning. She was tolerant of Campbell's variously silly questions and did her best with them. She did not do well, but it would have been hard to argue that her life demanded much more in the way of intellectual function than she enjoyed at present.

The other three were all in late middle age, and in their different ways neurotic rather than mentally impaired. A bachelor bank clerk seemed simply afraid of growing old. A housewife, perhaps, as she had noted herself, a victim of the 'empty nest', was worried by a variety of things, including her gradually increasing sherry intake. A man who had had something that sounded like a transient ischaemic attack was properly concerned that he might now be in for a full-blown stroke. Left to himself, Campbell would not have put any of them on treatment. The old lady was managing, and the scores of the three younger patients on simple mental testing left little room for improvement. However, since no one but a genius with lightning reflexes ever scored 100 per cent on the space invaders, the protocol allowed them to be included in the study, so they were enrolled for the various other tests, perhaps seeking the reassurance of normal results. Certainly none of them seemed to mind.

Drug evaluation was a funny business, Campbell reflected as he tidied up the files and took them along to reception. Perhaps treating people who didn't need treatment was one

73

of the standard ways of padding the results of a trial. If he passed the exam, he could always ring up Chief Backstay and see if the sea job with the helicopter training ship was still going. Meantime, he was in Edinburgh and his post, unofficially at least and even despite the sudden little rush of patients that morning, was sufficiently undemanding to be a useful study job.

'Where's Dunbar, David?'

'On the coast. About twenty miles out. Why?'

'Somebody rang from a nursing home there. They've got a place for Mrs Spence.'

'Oh. Does she need that?'

'Bobby must think she does.'

'What does she think?'

'I'm not sure she knows.'

'Wouldn't Bobby have discussed it with her?' Campbell was not entirely sure that he would have done.

'He hasn't been in for the last couple of days,' said Dr Phillips.

'No. He's abroad. Difficult.'

'When's he coming back?'

'Not sure.'

'So what do we do, David?'

'Hm. Do we have to do anything?'

'The woman said she couldn't guarantee the place unless she had word definitely today.'

Campbell had dropped into the ward for coffee, not to make difficult decisions.

'So what do we do?'

'What about the relatives.' Campbell thought of his old chief's quiet celebration at the club the previous evening.

'Nobody's been in to see her.'

'Perhaps someone'll come in this afternoon. If they're not going to have her home they really ought to discuss it with her themselves.'

'It's her house,' said Dr Phillips.

'Oh. Of course. Yes. Difficult.'

'Difficult.'

'What about the rest?'

'Well, you know Mr Lewis turned out to have motor neurone disease.'

'That's what it looked like. Does he know?'

'Dr Swift had a word with him.'

'Yes . . .' said Campbell. 'But does he know?'

Dr Phillips giggled and then looked thoughtful. 'Dr Swift sort of rattled on about the tests and all the things it probably wasn't but still might be.'

'I can imagine. Is he still in the ward? Mr Lewis.'

'Went home this morning. With an out-patient appointment for six months' time.'

'Oh. And that chap with multiple sclerosis?'

'He knows. He's looked it up. He wants to join their society and have that funny diet.'

'It doesn't work.'

'I know.'

'Anybody new?'

'A funny-turns lady from the waiting list. For the funny-turns work-up. And another of Bobby's private patients.'

'What?'

'Well, you know. A professor's father. Drinks. The letter says he's to have . . .'

'Auragen.'

Dr Phillips giggled again. 'You've guessed.'

'Who's the professor?'

'Who?'

'The professor the drunk's the father of.'

'Oh. Ear, nose and throat. A sort of jolly man with a moustache. Came in with his dad.'

'Oh, yes. Tubby Fuller.

'Is that what he's called? Bobby sort of collects professors' relatives, doesn't he?'

'Seems to.'

'Is it because he wants to be a professor himself?'

The answer most probably was yes. It occurred to Campbell that the sooner the composition of the interviewing committee for the neurology chair was known, the better.

Otherwise, there might be no end to the list of aunts, uncles, cousins, parents, siblings and friends of persons of possible influence who might pass through the ward and be put onto the big yellow tablets. On the other hand, the tribe of medicine worked in mysterious ways, and helping each other out with rather more than even a masonic selectivity was one of the hallmarks of its members. It was all rather difficult, but on balance, and if only because an evening with Hadden had left Campbell with more than his usual measure of cynicism, it now seemed that Dr Brown was overstepping the limits of mere comradeship and was veering into a perhaps risky exercise in self-advancement.

'. . . parenterovite as well?'

'Sorry?'

'I said if we put him on Auragen does he get parenterovite as well?'

'I suppose so. I mean, it's sort of standard. And something for his withdrawal too.'

'Heminevrin?'

'That would do. I'll see him later this afternoon. I've got some follow-ups from half past two.'

After lunch with Jo, Campbell went back to his office and found a brief note on his desk. It was handwritten, in pencilled capital letters, on a page of memo paper embossed in gold foil with 'Auragen: the Answer', and read 'DR CAMPBELL. SCORES IN PENCIL PLEASE. (DR JANKOWSKA ALWAYS USED PENCIL) R. FRANK.' He picked it up and walked quickly along the corridor to Dr Frank's room. It was locked and there was no answer to his knock.

He went on to the reception desk and asked Fiona if she had seen Dr Frank that day. She said she had not, but that in the past Dr Frank had sometimes been in the practice of looking in to the Unit briefly at lunchtime. Back in his room, he screwed up the note, threw it in the wastepaper basket and resolved to continue filling in the scoresheets in ink. Later, it might be interesting to discuss the matter with Dr Frank face to face.

*　　*　　*

'Doing fine thanks, doctor. Keeping much better, really. In fact, I feel great. Best I've felt in years.'

'And your memory?'

'A lot better. Like, I'm enjoying reading, the way I used to. For a while there I couldn't be bothered with stories, books and films on the television, like. I couldn't be bothered with them.'

'And your memory?'

'That's what I'm saying, doc. I can keep a hold of the story the way I used to. And that test was better. The one like space invaders.'

'Good.'

The man certainly looked well: young for his fifty-five years, and smartly turned out in rather a loud check suit with a flower in the buttonhole.

'Appetite all right?'

'Great. I really enjoy my food. Like, I didn't before.'

'And sleeping well?'

'Fine. Do the tablets make you sleep better, doc?'

'Hm. They might.'

'I was sleeping really badly a while back.'

'But better now?'

'A lot.'

'Good. Shall we try the paired-word test now, Mr Kitson?'

'Fine, doc.'

His responses were quick and accurate. Campbell, having no access to previous scores, wondered if and, if so, how much Mr Kitson's memory had actually improved.

'It's definitely better, doc.'

'Oh.'

'I got them all right, didn't I?'

'Yes.'

'I didn't before.'

Mr Kitson did the arithmetical tests quickly and confidently too, and at the end got up to go. 'Will I be seeing you again, doc? I mean, this seems to be the sort of place where you never see the same doctor twice.'

'How long have you been coming up, Mr Kitson?'

'This is just my second time. Cheers, doc. Maybe see you again.'

Campbell saw the man to the door, without committing himself to any future appointment. One never knew.

The next patient on the list, a Miss MacAffleck, was not around yet, so Campbell spent ten minutes or so brushing up on Oroya fever, an unusual infection transmitted by a South American mountain sandfly and therefore likely to be found only in the written part of the examination, although it was not entirely outwith the bounds of possibility that at the moment of truth one of the clinical examiners might smile pityingly and say, 'Well, Dr Campbell . . . if I were to tell you now that this man has just returned from a climbing holiday in the Andes . . . An important item that seems to have escaped your otherwise no doubt quite excellent clinical inquiries . . .' To be sure, he went over it twice.

Browsing among the various fevers, exotic and common-place, Campbell thought again about the patient he had just seen. Mr Kitson was in no doubt that the drug had improved his memory. Campbell went over his score sheets again, still with nothing from the previous attendance as a basis for comparison. Whatever his previous status, Mr Kitson was now doing well. Once more the question of access to previous records arose. Once more Campbell rang Dr Frank's number. Once more there was no answer.

The space-invaders test was administered by a part-time research assistant, a postgraduate psychologist who worked a few doors along the corridor. She was in her office, sitting reading a paperback historical romance.

'Dr Robson?'

She looked up, quite unembarrassed to be discovered thus. 'Come in.'

'Thanks. I've just seen a patient, a Mr Kitson . . .'

'Yes. I retested him this afternoon.'

'He thinks he's much better. Can you say? Do you have his old scores or anything?'

'No. I don't. I mean I just test people on that machine.' She indicated a formidable desktop computer with a large blank screen. 'And then note down the scores. He did quite well . . . I remember him from before though. He wasn't too bad. But better, a bit, this time.'

'Really?'

'Only a bit.'

'He seems quite keen on the stuff.'

'A lot of them are.'

'Are they?'

'Yes.' Dr Robson looked at Campbell in an odd sort of way. 'Yes. Some of them actually take a bigger dose than they're meant to.'

'Do they?'

'Yes. Have a seat, David. How was Mr Kitson on your tests?'

'All right. I mean, he was really quite good.'

'Did you ask him how much of the stuff he was taking?'

'No. I don't, usually.'

'You should.'

'Is that in the protocol?'

'No. It's just quite interesting to ask them.'

'D'you think it works?'

'You mean, on their memories?'

'Yes.'

'Difficult to say, with a study design like this. Comparing one dose with another when the patients tend just to dose themselves up anyway doesn't prove much either way.'

Campbell, who had previously met Dr Robson only briefly, and never talked with her about the drug or the study, was interested. She sounded as if she might be quite objective, in contrast with, for example, Dr Brown's rather wet-lipped enthusiasm for the allegedly miraculous properties of the substance they were testing.

'Do you think it works?' he asked again.

'Well, it must do something, or people wouldn't take more of it than they're supposed to.'

'I suppose so. But does it make their memories better? Have you looked at serial results, say of your space-invader stuff?'

Dr Robson sat back in her chair. 'The record system here's kind of funny.'

'I've just been trying to get hold of Dr Frank. Again.'

'You'll be lucky.' Dr Robson got up and closed the door of her office. 'Have you met her?'

'No. Have you?'

'Once. Not for long. When the Unit opened Bobby had us all upstairs in his office. She was there. She didn't actually stay long.'

'Oh.' Campbell realized that there were quite a few things he did not know about the Neurobiology Unit. He had not, for example, ever ventured upstairs, either invited or uninvited, to Dr Brown's office and laboratory suite. 'What's she like?'

'Fiftyish. Twitchy. Works funny hours. Shy.'

'What's her work like?'

Dr Robson shrugged. 'I don't see it.'

'Dr Brown said she's quite bright.'

'Hm. Hard to tell. Twitchy certainly. Bright maybe. I wouldn't know.'

'What did she do before she came here?'

'Not sure. Various things around the university and the Institute, mainly with numbers. I think with people she didn't get on with . . . And she's been in hospital for quite a while.'

'Really?'

'Yes.'

'Bobby mentioned something about her health.'

Dr Robson looked at Campbell as though deciding whether to go into details. There was a pause.

'It's all a bit odd,' said Campbell. 'Getting these results but not having any idea of how the patient's actually doing.'

'That's only because you're a doctor. You want to see them, and do things, and watch them get better and all that. That's why doctors make such bad scientists. They get involved, they get identified with things and lose their cool. For a study like this it's best just not to know too much. You should be simply doing the tests, hanging loose and letting the data tell the story, if there is a story.'

'I suppose so.' Campbell reflected on his shortcomings as a scientist.

'Dr Jankowska got very involved . . .'

'Did she?'

'Far too involved, even for a doctor. I shouldn't go on about her. It was all very sad and all that. But for her this study was . . . well, a crusade.'

'Really?'

'Yes. A sort of struggle against the forces of evil. With a bit of glory for herself thrown in . . . She'd care too much and get into all sorts of odd little relationships with the patients.'

That explained one or two things. 'I see,' said Campbell. 'I'd noticed some of them were more or less disappointed to see me.'

'Not one of your detached clinical investigators, our Theresa.'

'I didn't really know her.'

Dr Robson checked that her door was shut, was silent for a moment, then said, 'I think Dr Jankowska's death was more of a loss to medicine than it was to science.'

'I see.'

'I'm not sure the company would agree though.'

'The company?'

'Kristall Morgen. I think her enthusiasm went down quite well with them. You know. Nice positive results.'

'I see.'

'Which might eventually put you in a difficult position.' Dr Robson sat with her paperback in her hand, the epitome of scientific detachment.

'I hadn't really thought about that. I just took the job because it was there. I don't want to be a scientist or anything, but it might help get me through membership.'

'How did they find you?'

'Met Barry Swift in a pub. He said, "Dave, I've got just the job for you." '

'When was that?' Dr Robson was now a little less detached.

'Oh, only a couple of days after . . . the vacancy arose.'

'He is a shit.'

'Speak freely,' said Campbell. 'I'm not in his fan club or anything.'

'No. But Theresa was.'

'Didn't know that.'

'Yes. It was all a bit sad. Did you know her?'

'I knew who she was. Didn't know much about her.'

Dr Robson put down her book. 'I ended up knowing much more about her than I wanted to. She used to come in here and sit for ages, talking about Barry.'

'Really?'

81

'A bit sad. I mean, I felt quite sorry for her. You know Barry. A smug, shallow shit. Chats her up somewhere with his usual patter, and our Theresa overreacts, as with practically everything else she does, so it's girly chats about all sorts of things supershit Swift might have been a bit taken aback by. Pathetic, schoolgirl stuff really, coming from a twenty-whatever-year-old doctor. Do you know how she died?'

'Some sort of RTA?'

'She was driving home from her sister's wedding. Alone. And no other car involved either. Went off the road.'

'Drunk?'

'Might have been. It doesn't matter. The nasty bit is that old supershit had been all lined up to go to the wedding with her. Meet the family, partner the bridesmaid, etcetera, but he pulled out at the last minute.'

'Ugh.'

'A darts tournament.'

'Oh.'

Dr Robson looked out of the window, across the lawn to the Institute's clock tower. 'She was a mess, a little-girl, Middle-European mess. Made me feel awfully grown up. At first. Then she was boring. And then that.'

'And her work?'

'Enthusiastic, like I said. Too enthusiastic, really. When the Unit first opened she bounced around being the life and soul, ringing up GPs and making friends with the patients. A bit heavy for one or two of them, who stopped coming. And the same with the staff. Well, selectively. She hated Fiona, but spent hours and hours with Dr Frank. They used to go away together at weekends. That was before the Barry business started.'

'Interesting.'

'Oh, not that. At least I don't think so. More your thwarted-geniuses-together and aren't-men-horrible thing.' Dr Robson stopped suddenly and smiled. 'I shouldn't gossip. But Dr Frank's pretty odd, and so was Theresa, if that was what you were asking.'

'Thanks. Have you seen the other follow-up? Miss MacAffleck.'

'Not yet. I don't think she's here.'

'Well, mustn't keep you from your book. Thanks, Dr Robson.'

Campbell went back to his office and went through the desk and the filing cabinet, vetting all contents and reducing the material presence of the late Dr Jankowska to an odd little heap: a few plain white cards with lists of things to be done ('Mass. Dry-cleaning. Eggs. Bread'), some correspondence about a chain of prayer for some nuns in South America, and a few pens, together with a rather nice old silver or silver-plated propelling pencil which screwed apart to reveal a fluted cylindrical storage for spare leads and had a detachable cap covering an eraser.

He finished by taking down a calendar and a couple of wall posters, then speculated for a moment about his predecessor's parents, imagining an ageing and grief-stricken pair of half-acclimatized Middle Europeans. They might not want the shopping lists or the letters to their late daughter about tortured nuns, or the drug-company calendar with twelve views of the Alps, but the old-fashioned propelling pencil with its hidden eraser, perhaps the sort of thing they might have given their daughter years ago for some achievement in primary school, might be more welcome. With luck Dr Brown or his secretary upstairs would have their address.

In the continued absence of the second review patient, Campbell vastly increased his knowledge of the various causes of false positives in the standard tests for syphilis, and proceeded to the group of related but non-venereal disorders such as yaws, also known as framboesia and buba, and pinta, also known as carate and azul.

Bored eventually by rat-bite fever, he drifted along to the reception desk. Fiona, also evidently underemployed, seemed pleased to see him. He inquired again about Miss MacAffleck.

'She usually comes. She's small and wears funny hats.'

'With ''Kiss Me Quick'' and that sort of thing?'

'No. More glazed straw toques in navy blue with jade embellishments. That sort of thing. A very regular attender as a rule.'

'Oh . . . Who's her GP?'

'Fiona glanced at the file. 'Dr Gladhouse.'

'If she doesn't turn up I suppose I could ring him. If he's getting thirty pounds a month for his trouble . . . I'm going across to the ward for coffee.'

'D'you want me to ring if she comes.'

'I'll be back in ten minutes.'

'It was dreadful. I was clerking in a patient behind screens about three beds away and she was talking ever so loud. Shouting, in fact. He was talking quietly and trying to make her do the same, but she's a bit deaf so he couldn't really talk all that quietly. And I'm sure she wanted to embarrass him. I mean, everybody in the ward was listening.'

'What was she saying?'

'Oh, she was pretty fierce. ''Think I'm going gaga, do you? Trying to have me put away? Well, I'm telling you, young man'' – and I'm sure he's at least sixty – ''I'm telling you, young man, that it's my house and if anyone goes you do.'' '

'Embarrassing.'

'My patient loved it. She just sat there not listening to me and nodding every time Mrs Spence put him down. I could hardly stop myself laughing. Then a nurse came along and said, ''Mrs Spence, would you like to talk to your visitor in the interview room?'' That just made her worse. She said young people nowadays had no consideration and she didn't care who knew it. So he went away.'

'So what's happening?'

'Well, she's not going to Dunbar.'

'So I gathered.'

'And her lawyer's coming in tomorrow.'

'I see.'

'She was ever so angry. Do you take sugar, David?'

'No thanks. What's the new lady got?'

'Nothing very interesting. Vertebro-basilar insufficiency. She's booked for all the tests.'

'Otherwise OK?'

'Seems to be.'

84

'I'll go over her this afternoon if the review clinic over there's quiet. Is Barry around?'

Mrs Spence died quietly in her sleep that night. Two days later, when Dr Brown came back from Rumania, Campbell told him about it. He looked thoughtful then said 'She'd had a good innings. Ninety-six, wasn't it?'

'Ninety-five.'

'You didn't get a postmortem, did you?'

'We did.'

'That was a bit keen.'

'I thought it best to be on the safe side, and the daughter was quite happy about it. And since it was a sudden death in a previously fit lady . . .'

'Oh, strictly speaking you're absolutely right. And if it didn't distress the family . . .'

'It didn't.'

'I'd better ring Alester anyway, with my condolences. What did the PM show?

'Well, all the things she said she had, and quite extensive coronary artery disease. That's what we'd put on the death certificate.'

'Good . . . Well, I'll ring Alester at home this evening. How are the wards? Grand . . . I want to get on with these glucose uptake runs, and, of course, there's the backlog of administrative stuff. Remarkable how quickly it builds up. So it's just as well all's quiet.'

Campbell could not immediately see how the quietness or otherwise of wards he rarely visited directly affected Dr Brown's routine, but rather than say so he asked about Rumania.

'Wonderful place, David. Ever been there yourself?'

'No.'

'Not even with the navy? No. I suppose not. But really, a wonderful place, and the food's quite good in the bigger tourist hotels. They do wonderful things with lamb, and the local plonk's quite good in its own way, if you're into the heavier sorts of red. And, of course, the famous Professor

85

Dr Elena has all the right contacts, so we really ate very well. How's the Unit? Anything in the way of new patients?'

'Nine in the past week.'

'That's pretty good. Just goes to show that even the most conscientious people need reminding. You've got to hand it to Mike Forrest. He's really got a gift for that sort of thing.'

'How's the Rumanian end of things?'

Dr Brown smiled. 'Quite . . . influential.'

'Influential?'

'Professor Dr Elena's got half the government on Auragen. That's fair enough, I suppose. About half our lot would probably benefit from it too. Elena's very persuasive, and you know what these Eastern European governments are like. Average age around eighty. And, as Elena says, ''Eeet's vonderful stoff, in every vay . . . Or so their meestresses tell me.'' ' Dr Brown chuckled at this new and welcome attribute of Auragen. 'And, of course, it's vital from the international scientific point of view to make sure that the Eastern Bloc countries feel they're included. So it was well worth the three or four days away from the lab.' Dr Brown reached over and picked up a copy of *Short Notes on Postgraduate Medicine*. 'And how's the membership swotting coming along?'

'It's all a bit alarming.'

'That's a useful wee book. One or two quite important omissions in the neurology section, but we can go over them together nearer the time.'

'Thank you. Dr Brown, there was another death.'

'On the ward?'

'No. One of the outpatients.'

'From the neurology clinic?'

'No. The Unit. One of the evaluation patients. On Auragen.'

'Someone I'd seen?'

'I'm really not sure. A Miss MacAffleck. A patient of Dr Gladhouse. She didn't turn up so I rang him. He said he hadn't seen her himself for a couple of months but would check her records, then he rang me back to say she'd died. In church, it seems.'

'Aged?'

86

'Seventy-one.'

'Suddenly?'

'Brought in dead to casualty. I got out her notes, but they didn't help much.'

Dr Brown looked thoughtful, then said, 'Well, I suppose it would be too much to hope that Auragen confers the gift of eternal life.'

Campbell was a little surprised by that. 'I thought I should mention it. Just in case there was any . . .'

Dr Brown smiled. 'Come on, David. Two old ducks, average age eighty-four . . .'

'I just wondered . . .'

'That's one of the things we went over in detail with Kristall Morgen right at the start. I don't know how much you know about drug evaluation, David. Most companies are a lot less fussy. I told them that inevitably the patients in the trial would be getting on a bit in years, and that we'd have deaths on treatment simply because now that typhoid, cholera and childbed fever are out it's the older people who, quite properly, so to speak, are doing the dying. Obviously. Yes, they said, we know most companies try to exclude old people from their trials because of this, but we know this drug's going to be used mainly on older folks, so we're going to be completely honest about evaluating it. And, as you know, David, we monitor for liver and kidney damage, and every patient is seen, at considerable expense to the company, both by us and by their own general practitioner. So nothing, but nothing, is going to slip through unnoticed. But we can't go around promising that eighty-four-year-olds are going to live for ever.' Dr Brown paused, then said, 'Obviously, we record these . . . incidents, and bear in mind the faint possibility that it's anything to do with Auragen, but that's all we need do for now. As Elena says, "Eeet's vonderful stoff." The job now is to document that, quantify it with good data from a big series.'

Dr Brown slid heavily from his worktop perch to the floor. His complexion combined a faint suntan and an inner glow perhaps most recently attributable to Rumanian claret. As he moved to the door, Campbell noticed a line of sweat across his upper lip. With one hand on the door handle he paused again. 'And you're all set up for the symposium in Rhodes, David?'

'Hm?'

'Be a nice break for you, after membership. And a chance for you to present some of the Edinburgh data.'

Campbell continued to look blank. Dr Brown smiled. 'I must surely have mentioned the Eastern Mediterranean Symposium to you, David . . . Well, perhaps not. Anyway, it'll be just what you need after membership. A week away from the shop, a good hotel and a chance to do your stuff with your data. And, of course, it'll be published, probably as a special supplement to the *Journal of Clinical and Metabolic Neurology*. Just the sort of publication you need at this stage. I'll send the symposium bumph down to you. The programme's still a bit flexible so it'll be no trouble to give you a fifteen-minute slot. Probably with Elena in the chair . . . It's no trouble, David, no trouble at all. The very least we could do for you, considering all you've done for us. And you'll even have the pleasure of meeting the famous Professor Dr Elena. Grand . . . grand, David. And the wards are all right?'

'Seem to be.'

'Good. And that wee girl from Manchester settling in?'

Campbell thought about that, then, trying not to sound too interested, said that she probably was. The previous night he and Dr Phillips had gone together to a show on the Festival Fringe. After ninety minutes of a heavily adapted version of *Hedda Gabler*, done by an all-female cast in red overalls as lesbian protest theatre, they had left early and gone back to the residency. Campbell, who had not visited that part of the hospital in the two years since he himself had been a houseman, had lingered sentimentally over the group photographs on the stairway, looking for his own vintage. Dr Phillips, a few steps above him, had held out her hand and said, 'Come on, David.'

'. . . Dr Frank?'

'Sorry, Dr Brown.'

Dr Brown, genial and relaxed about a lapse of attention on the part of one of his assistants, repeated the question. 'And you're getting on all right with Dr Frank?'

'Well, I've been giving her the results as I get them . . . Just putting them through her door. I mean, I still haven't seen her.'

'She really copes remarkably well. We should all be very grateful to her . . . That's grand, David. As I said, I'll be fairly busy for the next couple of days . . . But my door upstairs is always open.'

'I might have been quite worried about you, not knowing where you were. It's just not like you. I mean, you always come home at night. I could have been worried about you. I might even have phoned your mum. Or the Rose Street police box.'

'You didn't.'

'Of course I didn't.'

'But you weren't there last night either.'

'No. But if I had been I would have been worried. You just weren't there when I went back for a clean shirt after the ward round. Who is she, then? Do I know her?'

'I don't think so. What about you?'

'Duty. But it wasn't lonely. And you know her. The staff nurse on nights in thoracic. Used to be in casualty when we were there.' Bones leered and took a gulp of his beer. 'Dark hair. Brown eyes. Big and sort of athletic about it.'

'When you were both on duty?'

'Came up to see me in the registrar's bedroom at her mealbreak. Told me how all the patients were doing and gave me a share of her yoghurt. Afterwards. And she thinks she can get a swop so she's on at the weekend with me. It's funny. I never liked yoghurt before. I think I'll start buying it for the flat. For when she comes over.'

'So it's love.'

'What about you? Come on. Do I know her? Is it that Jean bird again. The one that makes all the noise. God, I hope not. I couldn't stand it. I'd leave. I need my sleep, you know.'

'Don't worry.'

'So it's a new one?'

'Yes.'

'A staff nurse? Or have you started on ward sisters? That one on your female ward? The one with flat feet.'

'No.'

89

'Come on. Don't be shy. Is it someone you know from the navy? A midshipman maybe? I don't mind, you know. Flatmates have to be pretty tolerant these days. You can tell me if you want to. But you don't have to. Is he nice? I mean, I'd understand, after you being off all-boys-together for months at sea. I really wouldn't mind. And if he's got any ideas about soft furnishings for the lounge . . .'

'Sorry,' said Campbell. 'You don't know her.'

'Her? Well, that's a relief.'

'Nice girl. Resident on the ward.'

'A houseperson? So . . . You were back in the residency?'

Campbell nodded.

'It's funny,' said Bones. 'I was thinking about that the other day. It's like school. You just don't go back. What was it like?'

'Like school. You know. The pictures. And the smell.'

'And people screwing next door?'

'Not last night. But I'm getting a bit old for single beds.'

'Is she fat?'

Campbell decided it might be simplest to introduce Bones and Jo when the opportunity arose, and talk meantime of other things. 'How's thoracic?'

'Well, nights on call are looking up.'

'And apart from that?'

'Weekends on call. Oh, I meant to ask you. We did a guy this afternoon. Hacked out his thymoma. All jolly carpenters together and having a nice time chipping away and then somebody started a silly conversation about how many per cent of them get myasthenia gravis. Silly really, for surgeons, but the Prof got quite professorial and he must have just been reading it up to impress us because he was going on and on about Eaton-Lambert inverse myasthenia and stuff. D'you know about that?'

'No.'

'But they might ask you about it in membership.'

'They might.'

'Then they would ask you about who Eaton and Lambert were. Or Eaton-Lambert if it was just one chap with a double-barrelled name.'

'I suppose so. What is it?'

'How should I know? I'm just the man that chops out the thymomas. But if you came across it with all this reading you're doing you could tell me. How long is it now?'

'Three weeks.'

'Are you getting scared.'

'I'd like to get it out of the way.'

'How many times do they let you have a go at it?'

'Six, I think. You get a book of tickets when you pass the first part, and you send one off with your money for second part. I think it's six.'

'That should probably be enough,' said Bones. 'I mean, if you're going to get it at all. Where are you sitting it this time?'

'Leith hospital. That's the clinical. All the rest's at the college.'

'Funny place, Leith. The physicians there have got all these weird things they save up for membership exams. They had it when I was there as a student. Some real rocking-horse shit. Familial pendular nystagmus was one. Do you know about that?'

'No.'

'Well, you've got plenty of time to look it up.'

'Thanks.'

'I'd like to see you get through first time. Then maybe you'd get a decent job . . . People ask me what you're doing these days, and I'm fed up explaining about that place and why you haven't got a proper job.'

'Really?'

'People seem to think the Neurobiology Unit's a bit weird.'

'It is.'

'Is it? That fat chap, the boss, does funny brain research, doesn't he?'

'Yes. He's got a lab upstairs.'

'What's it like? Bubbling vats of mashed brains and machines that only work when it's dark and the moon's full?'

'I wouldn't know. I've never been up there. Might be, I suppose.'

'If I were him I'd be working towards brain trans-plantation. I really doubt if the physicians are ever going to make any progress on dementia. And they've been at it for years. If there's an answer, it'll be surgical, like so many other things. He's probably got dozens of brains up there in liquid nitrogen, just waiting to be popped in and wired up when we get a proper microvascular service . . . Have you asked him what he's actually up to?'

'He's doing something on brain metabolism. He sort of chats about glucose uptake, but seems to be able to come and go a fair bit. He was in Rumania earlier this week. It's a multicentre trial, mainly in nice places. I think he goes to Aix-en-Provence and Tijuana as well.'

'Where's that?'

'Mexico. Near California. And they're having a conference on Rhodes soon.'

'Rhodes?'

'In Greece.'

'You going?'

'Looks like it.'

Bones thought about that then said, 'Greek women are kind of hairy and don't, but there's always stacks of secretaries on package tours. Might be a bit late for them but you never know. Stuart Shawlands was in Corfu last September and he had a fantastic time. Apparently there were these two secretaries from Sheffield, kind of old but . . .'

A couple of pints later they left the pub, Bones to a rendez-vous with his newfound love, Campbell back to their flat in Marchmont. The evening was cool and moist, dusk notice-ably earlier than only a week before. A Fringe show audience straggled from a church hall with an air of painful duty over. At the top of Middle Meadow Walk a bank of early leaves had drifted against the traffic island. The Institute, vast and close, huddled within its walls like a medieval town, seemed sud-denly inviting. Campbell recalled his various uncertainties about the finer points of myasthenia gravis and decided on impulse to go to his office and read it up.

The hospital was quiet. He walked across the courtyard and along almost the whole length of the medical corridor without meeting anyone. As he passed the various ward entrances, a succession of little cameos of hospital life was on offer: a nurse doing a medicine round; an auxiliary with a trolley of hot drinks; a patient in his dressing gown, helping. It was only as he turned from the main corridor Campbell realized that he did not have a key to the Neurobiology Unit, and it was by no means certain that it would be open. He tried the door gently, glancing round on the off chance that one of the Institute's motley and predominantly drunk array of security personnel might see him and draw the wrong conclusions. The door opened. Inside, the air was warm and still and smelled of new carpet.

The light switch was not obviously accessible. Campbell stood for a moment then began to walk across the reception area and towards his office. He was startled by a noise at the top of the stair, a soft dry shuffling sound, and he glanced upwards. A vaguely human shape was silhouetted against the skylight. The shuffling stopped briefly, then resumed, and the figure moved to stand at the top of the stair. Campbell stayed where he was, in shadow by the reception desk, uncertain as to whether he had discovered an intruder or whether he himself was about to be identified as one. The figure moved into a patch of light on the upper part of the stair, so that Campbell could see it better, though he still could not distinguish much about its clothing or indeed its gender. Apart from the shuffle, the oddest thing visible so far was the hair, a tangle of long and untidy curls hanging and protruding in all directions. With one hand on the banister, the figure proceeded downstairs; angular, of medium height and clad in trousers and a long-sleeved shirt or blouse. Closer, it was more obviously female. There was no indication that whoever it was had seen Campbell. She stared fixedly ahead, stiffly grasping the banister with one hand, holding a sheaf of papers in the other. Descending slowly, one step at a time, she reached the bottom step and turned first towards Campbell, then past him, still evidently without seeing him. The face was masklike, the gaze fixed ahead, the overall impression one of inner misery and turmoil, possibly half contained by drugs.

Stiff, bedraggled and slow, the figure receded. Campbell sniffed the air and then held his breath. An odour, partly a cheap and awful perfume and partly something far, far worse, the stench of months and months of fetid self-neglect, hung pungently in the warm darkness long after the figure had disappeared into the office in which Campbell had on several occasions but never hitherto successfully sought his colleague Dr Frank.

PART THREE

By the time Campbell found the Tansey Street practice he realized he must have driven past it perhaps two or three times. The district, a series of decaying Georgian blocks on the northern margin of the New Town, was unfamiliar, and Dr Brown's directions had been far from clear. He parked his car and walked back to the practice, which occupied a large ground-floor flat and was marked from the outside only by a dingy brass plate and a faded notice saying 'No Parking: Doctors' Cars Only: Day and Night'.

In the hallway there were two rows of assorted bentwood chairs and an official notice discouraging requests for home visits. No patients waited. Behind a sliding glass panel in a partition a woman of middle age sat smoking and knitting. Campbell stood for a moment on the square of worn linoleum in front of the hatch, politely assuming he would be noticed when she had finished the row. As he was not, he pressed a bell marked 'Ring for Attention'. The woman put down her knitting and swept the glass panel aside, so that a pall of smoke belched out into his face. She coughed and asked, 'Have you got an appointment?'

Up to that moment Campbell had rather assumed that he had. Now he wasn't so sure. Dr Brown's guidance as to the nature and details of the mission had been almost as vague as his street directions. As he had explained, he would have gone himself had he not been called away suddenly to Aix-en-Provence. But he had not explained anything else very clearly. The only really firm point that had emerged was that in the suddenly changed circumstances Campbell should go in his place.

The Tansey Street practice was, it appeared, a major source of referrals for the Auragen study and might, it appeared, be the source of many more. Not that Dr Brown would have attempted anything so crude as touting for new patients for his Neurobiology Unit. He had stressed that point as a major item of professional propriety. It was more a question, as he had put it, of 'keeping in touch', 'letting people know we're still interested' and, of course, 'making sure that everyone concerned is really keeping an eye open for side-effects', drug safety having evidently become a new and major concern of Dr Brown.

'Well?' said the woman. 'Do you have an appointment?'

'I think so,' said Campbell. 'It's about the Auragen study.'

'Is that a new drug?'

Campbell nodded. The woman coughed and said, 'The partners don't usually see drug company representatives during consulting hours, though it's possible you might get an appointment in about six months . . . if you write in.' She coughed again and picked up a small and well-thumbed maroon-covered desk diary. 'However, they sometimes see people over lunch . . . Denzler's or Prestonfield House?' She had opened the diary and was waiting for Campbell's reply.

'It was probably Dr Brown's secretary who made the appointment. For Dr Brown. From the Institute. Unfortunately he's been called away . . .'

The woman glanced at Campbell as though he had deliberately caused her much unnecessary trouble. 'So you're not a drug rep?'

'No.'

'And you think Dr Brown arranged for you to see the partners?'

'I think it was mainly Dr McVittie.' What Dr Brown had actually said was 'It's mainly a question of keeping old Jim McVittie sweet . . . Without actually twisting his arm for more patients.'

'I'm not sure if he's still around.' The woman coughed again, put down her cigarette, smiled at Campbell to emphasize that she was doing him a great favour, and retreated into the dark interior of the premises.

'Thank you, Mrs Connagher. Perhaps Dr Campbell would like some coffee . . . Yes? Good. Thank you, Mrs Connagher.'

The receptionist coughed her way back along the corridor and Campbell took the seat indicated, beside the untidiest desk he had ever seen. There were four or five penholders, each branded with a drug name and bristling with similarly branded throwaway pens, together with half a dozen drug-emblazoned notepads and a vast clutter of various other gifted items such as staplers, paperclip holders and little cans of airfreshener. Drifts of junk mail, opened and unopened, extended in all directions from the one clear space, an area in the middle at the front just big enough to take a prescription pad or a cup and saucer. Dr McVittie lounged back in his swivel chair. 'I was sorry to miss Bobby's dinner out at the Pelicans. Had one the same night in town that I'd signed up for months before. Unfortunately. But I think the practice was represented. And how's Bobby?'

'As I said, he's had to go off to one of the other centres, and . . .'

'Busy man, Bobby. Always doing things. He'll make an excellent professor, given half a chance. Never seen such a chap for pushing back the frontiers. Drug trials . . . symposia . . . and all those publications . . . Is it true he's done about a hundred and fifty? Never seen anything like it. And, of course, down here at Tansey Street we're always happy to help. Maintain the academic link . . . Easy for you chaps up at the Institute to get out of touch, and we're always happy to help.' Dr McVittie paused, but not for long enough for Campbell to feel he could contribute. 'Of course, things have changed beyond recognition over the last thirty years. Students? Never saw them in the old days. Now they're here practically all the time. Four weeks, no less, in their fourth or

97

fifth year. That's a great advance. So that by the time they qualify they've had their feet on the ground for a month at least. It's funny, we don't seem to have had so many of them lately, but I suppose they're trying to spread the load . . . Ah, thank you, Mrs Connagher. Most kind. Sugar? No? I'm sure you're right, but I've always taken it, so what's the point of changing at my age. And carrying a bit of weight doesn't seem to do any harm. Up to a point . . . Though moderation in all things, hm?'

Campbell nodded. Dr McVittie sipped his coffee, smiled, then said, 'I think the last time I saw Bobby was in Malaga, at a symposium on hypnotics in general practice. We'd done some of the evaluation. He really is a remarkable chap. And how is he?'

The question had caught Campbell with his coffee at his lips, and by the time he had removed it the chance to answer had passed again. Dr McVittie twinkled and said, 'Of course, we wish him well in this current study. I believe one or two of us have patients taking part, and some of them might even be doing quite well, but . . .'

Dr McVittie paused and lowered his spectacles a little, so that he was looking over them rather than through them: a gesture which seemed to Campbell to be a studied prelude to some major statement ('I'm afraid the news from the specialist is not at all good . . .').

'Dr Campbell . . .'

'Yes?'

'Dr Campbell, you're too young to remember how we managed things before nineteen forty-eight . . .'

Campbell nodded.

'So it must be quite difficult for you to really appreciate the basis upon which we do things. Practice . . . and consultation. The relationship between those of us who are providers of care, and those who provide simply advice. Because that's all it is, you know. And to say that is in no way to detract from the service that chaps like Bobby provide for us. But it is only advice. Take that drug of yours, for instance. It may be all very well in its way, but it's only one of a number of drugs in the field. I don't know how much you know about some of the

98

other drugs.' Dr McVittie indicated a large glossy calendar hanging to the right of his desk. It depicted a roseate autumnal sunset into which, along a woodland path, an elderly couple strolled hand in hand. A caption in letters larger than those indicating the month proclaimed 'For the elderly . . . Geritabs' and underneath, in letters only slightly smaller, 'And Geritabs Forte . . . for the constipated elderly'.

When Campbell had had a moment to familiarize himself with the details of the rival drug, Dr McVittie smiled and said, 'We retain our clinical independence, you know. That much we snatched from Bevan and the flames.' He got up. Campbell, surprised to find the interview evidently at an end, got up too. 'Thank you for coming along, Dr Campbell. Awfully good to keep in touch. And my best to Bobby. Particularly about the chair. So very difficult sometimes, isn't it?'

'Your first shot?'

'Yes . . . Yours?'

'Not quite. Third, actually.'

'Oh.'

'Twice in London. So I thought I'd come back here and at least fail it among friends. Quite a party, isn't it? George Collins is here somewhere. And remember Larry Prossor. Odd little chap with a stammer who failed biochem. I never really knew him but he was in our year. And Helen. Helen's over there looking obnoxiously confident.'

'She always did.'

'Ah, yes. But I know for a fact this isn't her first time either. She was there in London last time I tried.'

'Really?'

'Yes. So was that little Chinese chap from Mauritius.'

'Kim?'

'Yes. He was there too. I think he passed.'

'What's he doing now?'

'Something clever at the Brompton. Where's Helen?'

'Just started in Botley's unit. Starred for glory, I suppose. What about you?'

'Oh, I'm playing at being a gastroenterologist. For the time being at least. The pancreas is quite interesting. And you?'

'Oh, just a locum. A drug-money job in neurology. It's for membership really.'

'So you're not going to stay in neurology?'

'I don't think so.'

'Pretty tight for jobs, isn't it?'

'Yes. And it's a bit gloomy. Most of the patients don't do well.'

'Who was that chap who used to say "Medicine gives me something to do in the mornings"?'

'Struthers.'

'He's in neurology. Registrar at Queen's Square.'

'Good luck to him.'

'Well, it's the sort of specialty where being like Struthers probably helps quite a lot. At least in London . . . Oh.'

'Yes . . . Well, good luck.'

'And you.'

About a hundred and fifty variously young and middle-aged doctors, of all colours from deepest ebony to panic-stricken clammy white, crowded from the foyer of the college into its examination hall. Campbell and his classmate, one Murray, were separated by a pale Indian or Pakistani, greenish yellow with apprehension, who had four pens and three pencils in his top pocket. Murray continued to behave as if this were mainly a social function. He smiled and nodded to acquaintances and courteously made way for people more anxious or hurried than himself. As he and Campbell struck out through the crowd in search of the previously allocated numbered desks, he signalled with a brief gesture, as though lifting a full glass to his lips, and mouthed the words 'Five o'clock.' Campbell nodded and Murray acknowledged this with a thumbs-up. Perhaps that was the best way to view the written section of part two of the membership examination: something to do until the pubs opened.

The bustle of desk-finding over, a deep peace settled upon the examination hall. Row upon row of candidates sat silent for those first sacramental moments when the paper is read and the questions are revealed. In front, an invigilator in a dusty black robe stood with the apologetic air of a prison chaplain in the execution shed, more useful for his symbolic presence than for anything he might actually do. From the walls a couple of dozen heavily framed oil portraits of the distinguished and the merely office-bearing invigilated too.

One Andrew Duncan, a gentle old man perhaps portrayed by Raeburn, seemed to look with especial kindness on that part of the hall where Campbell sat between a Chinaman and some sort of Arab, the former managerially impassive, jotting notes as though passing the time on a transoceanic flight, the latter sighing softly to himself or his god, and writhing and rubbing his eyes. It dawned on Campbell that he was in that fortunate minority sitting the examination in his native language.

Comfortably settled in, he turned his mind to a more detailed appraisal of what had seemed at first sight five not unreasonable cases for discussion. One, concerning an obscure metabolic problem in a newborn child, could be discarded straightaway. Of the remaining four, he had to tackle three. This being the second part of the examination, the cases were intentionally and expectedly less than straightforward. Part one of the membership, a vast array of multiple-choice questions, had purported to test factual knowledge. Now the examiners sought to test something other than the ability to recall pieces of textbook. Case histories, garnished with perhaps significant detail ('A forty-eight-year-old single barman, recently returned from holiday in Spain, complains of malaise and a painful left ankle . . .') were followed by a fusillade of laboratory findings ('Hb 11.2 gms, ESR 43 mms in 1st hr, MCV 104 . . .').

From the instructions, and from the popular wisdom circulating among junior hospital doctors, it was known that no single answer would suffice. The barman, for example, might be suffering from rheumatic fever, gonorrhea, tuberculosis or any one of a host of variously unfortunate or retributive pathologies. The trick seemed to be to entertain physicianly doubts at a level at once both based in probabilities and reflecting an extensive knowledge of medicine, the instructions implying rather than stating that marks would be deducted from candidates appearing to make up their minds.

The Oriental on the left, his preliminary jottings over, had begun to write steadily. The Arab, who had managed only a few despairing squiggles on the inside cover of the examination book, sank over his desk, head cradled in folded arms and pointing, with any luck, towards Mecca: certainly more or less east along Queen Street. The invigilator in black, an aged college Fellow with a hearing aid and glasses of the sort provided after cataract surgery, sat now at a table overlooking the hall from a dais. A clock ticked softly above him. One and a quarter hours to go.

In his revision for the exam Campbell had been constantly surprised by items of medical knowledge of which he had been previously only vaguely aware and which explained or clarified various untidy bits of his clinical experience: nothing quite so gross as 'So that's what she died of: wish I'd thought of it', but a series of illuminating clinical associations that made sense of superficially unrelated phenomena, and if his reading had not made him much of a diagnostician, it had at least made him more aware of the processes involved. Most of medicine, it now seemed, was pattern recognition. Nature tossed you two or three things in the clinical presentation, you looked for another few the patient hadn't drawn your attention to, sensing already a half-completed picture, like the children's game of joining the numbered dots, during which an eyebrow or a snout emerges and suddenly the whole thing becomes clearer. The best diagnosticians seemed to be the people who, by knowledge and experience, got the picture quickest from the fewest dots.

For the exam, cases were chosen which were deliberately vague: not quite enough dots for clarity, but enough to exert the candidate to go into detailed speculation in the area specified. You assumed, for example, that a single forty-eight-year-old barman would drink a fair bit, especially on holiday, and might also have been tempted by the sirens, male or female, of the holiday beaches. And you were supposed to know that barmen had a higher than average incidence of TB. Then you cast around with that, and the scatter

102

of undefinitive laboratory information offered, and did your best.

Hadden had once said that you should not embarrass the examiners by raising things they didn't know about. If you sounded sensible they tried to pass you and if you sounded brilliant they were out to put you down. A diagnostic computer, and a certain sort of junior hospital doctor, usually from abroad, could no doubt have produced a list of several hundred possibilities for the barman and his troubles. Campbell couldn't. He thought of three more or less likely answers, then, with a bit of an effort, another, and a fifth considerably less likely. That would have to do, and he ended up having written only a page and a half before going on to the next case. As he did so, a little Indian in a shiny blue suit got up and walked to the back of the hall for more paper, having presumably covered the eight sides of foolscap first provided.

The second case history concerned a middle-aged woman who had suffered some sort of neurological disaster: the sort of thing Campbell had seen occasionally as a casualty officer. Then it had been quite simple: you asked the neurosurgeons to see the case. When they had decided it wasn't anything they could do anything about, you passed it on to the physicians, who watched and waited until some development permitted further investigation, if only a postmortem. Under exam conditions, however, a more rigorously theoretical approach was required. The case did not prove anything like as congenial to deal with as the barman, and Campbell left it with only a bit less than a page of rather muddled thought committed to paper.

He then had to decide which of the remaining two cases would do less harm to his chances of passing: the lorry driver with abdominal symptoms or the old lady with persistent pain in her right shoulder. On balance, the lorry driver offered more scope for the sort of educated speculation required, as Campbell had once spent six months in the shallow end of clinical gastroenterology as part of a research job, and cases such as this had regularly turned up as out-patients. Broadly speaking, there were two nice and three nasty causes of that sort of thing, one of the latter being very nasty indeed.

In out-patients you could ask and prod. In the churchlike isolation of the examination hall you could only wonder, but a couple of pages of perhaps passable stuff resulted. At the end of the first hour, by which time it seemed that about half the candidates had made the pilgrimage to the back of the hall to ask for more paper, Campbell still had several blank pages in his book.

In the second hour a new invigilator appeared and distributed fresh booklets, which contained a series of data-interpretation problems. This time there were no stories, just trackless wastes of laboratory results which did not run to flesh-and-blood details, except in the most literal sense. Under the oil paintings the hundred and fifty or so candidates wrestled with low calciums, high phosphates, poikilocytosis, neutrophilia, hypoxaemia, C-21 hydroxylase deficiency and a host of similarly encoded messages from the machinery of modern medicine. Would Andrew Duncan, whom Campbell supposed vaguely to be an early specialist in the yet unnamed specialty of psychiatry, have been interested to know that an increased excretion of urinary aminolevulinic acid and faecal coproporphyrins was associated with porphyria, the most likely cause of the possibly contemporaneous George III's recurrent madness?

At four the congregation was invited to rise and file into the college lecture theatre for the third part of the written section of the second part of membership, in which a series of slides were shown, candidates answering related questions listed in yet another examination booklet. To Campbell, some of the things shown were, if not familiar, at least vaguely recognizable. Others, on the margin of his knowledge, were perhaps usefully guessable, the remainder completely uninformative. Sometimes, as a slide went up, there was a little frisson of audience reaction. An X-ray of an abdomen with a calcified arterial abnormality the size of a turnip elicited an awestruck intake of breath, and at one point someone was sufficiently carried away by his delight at recognizing the higher significance of some bluish purple chilblains on a young woman's nose and cheeks as to emit a short elated giggle. But for the most part the slides came and went in semidarkness and a silence broken only by the rustle of paper and the scratch of pens.

When the lights finally went up and the examination booklets had been gathered in, there was a general move back to the foyer. Friends and even strangers consoled or encouraged one another, suddenly voluble on the expiry of their vow of silence. Campbell made his way through the throng of dark suits, overhearing as he went one or two fragments. 'Type two.' 'Rarely seen in the absence of sarcoidosis.' 'It was a sarcoma . . . She had Paget's.' 'Gee, shit. Diphyllobothrium latum . . .' 'Osler-Weber-Rendu, unless I am much mistaken . . .' 'Myxoedema . . . Bloody hell. Yes.' Some of it was encouraging, some dispiriting. Campbell looked round for Murray, and realized that almost all his previous experience of medical exams had been collective rather than individual. As an undergraduate you charged in a horde, knowing that in the weight of numbers you would make it, if only because they needed housemen. Now, if you were lucky, there were a few people around whom you knew, and most of you would fail.

Some candidates stood alone, exhausted by three hours' conclusive effort about which they might have been worrying for months. Others, perhaps acquaintances only from the exam circuit, chatted in groups, comparing answers and jotting down questions for future reference. With five of the all-important little pink tickets left in his book, Campbell felt that it would be unsought-for but fortunate to pass. What did it feel like to have only two tickets left, or none?

'Oh, better than the first time, I suppose. But not as good as the second. You?'

'Hm. Interesting. The data-interpretation bit was the worst.'

'Yes. It's a bit more like part one. It's all in the books, if you know the books.'

'Well . . . Perhaps next time. What was that leg supposed to be?'

'I thought erythema induratum, but I couldn't remember what you get it with.'

'TB.'

'Oh, well . . . Cheers anyway.'

'Cheers.'

'Here's to the next time.'

Murray and Campbell had walked a couple of blocks up the hill to a bar just off St Andrews Square chosen by Murray as very much the sort of place to have a drink if you're not up in Edinburgh for long. It certainly seemed to suit him. His general style, that of a good chap from a good regiment out on the town in mufti, went nicely with the brass-and-mahogany heaviness, and the panels of engraved mirror.

It was a bar of which Campbell had known nothing until it had been threatened with destruction to make way for more sock counters for an adjoining department store. The ensuing campaign had not only saved it, as was proper, but had evoked a whole new clientele. It was certainly an impressive place to take people with the standard view on Scottish pubs. The Victorian bar furnishings, unmodernized, lent respectability, solemnity even, to pub-going. Six tall stained-glass windows portrayed manly sporting pursuits in the dress of the nineties, with the cricketer and footballer well wrapped up against the stern Caledonian air. Even the cash registers were traditional clanging brass.

One trivial item marred it for Campbell. On the end wall a vast ceramic seascape with an early steamer, contained a visual irritant, possibly a minor error by a tradesman, enshrined now for the best part of a century. One tile, near the bottom left-hand corner, in a grey-green foreground of overcast, choppy sea, was almost certainly upside down. It was not important, or even particularly obvious, but once you had noticed it it was infinitely distracting, perhaps more so after a couple of pints: one tile, out of hundreds, that might have been intended the other way up, so that the lighter green wavetop would continue uninterrupted through to the edge of the picture.

'. . . back to London.'

'Oh. Yes. What train are you getting.'

'The six o'clock. So time for one or two more. What did you think was wrong with the old lady?'

'Not sure. Didn't try her. Thought about it and couldn't get much beyond maybe polymyalgia, or a secondary from a tumour I couldn't work out.'

'I wondered about gall bladder. You can get pain referred to shoulder. But that's the trouble with gastroenterology. Makes you terribly narrow-minded.'

'I didn't think of that.'

'Of course, in real life she'd have arthritis, but I suppose the college couldn't take your money and just ask about that.'

Along the bar a group of youngish people, mainly women, out on some sort of office celebration, waxed noisy over the second round. Loud, confident and uncouth, they seemed to Campbell, at least when he was in the company of Murray, to represent the new barbarism at least as vigorously as the proposed but defeated sock department. From their accents, vocabulary and snatches of conversation it was reasonable to assume that they were social workers, mainly first-generation graduates of working-class origin. Most of the women were smoking. One, with dry, dark-red hair, remarked during a sudden silence, to a bearded male companion, 'If I'm into anything, I'm into maself.' Campbell eavesdropped a little, while Murray was getting another round, and was hugely gratified to hear them discussing which was the best place to be sick at a party.

The bar filled slowly and became pleasantly busy. At about half past five Campbell was surprised to notice, at the end of the bar, beyond the social workers and more or less under the offending tile, the solitary, substantial figure of Dr Brown, sitting on a bar stool and nursing a gin and tonic. It was unusual to see consultants in public bars in Edinburgh: sufficiently so for Campbell to have resolved that, if ever the fates were to bestow or inflict upon him a senior appointment locally, he would more or less stop. Dr Brown did not appear to have seen his junior colleague, nor was he obviously avoiding him. He sat rather sadly, alone, quite unlike his usual, social self. Campbell wondered first whether Dr Brown was in the habit of drinking alone, and secondly whether he might have an appointment of a kind it might be tactful to ignore. Certainly the bar could be seen as having had that sort of atmosphere, and was well off the usual circuit for Institute people.

Campbell was still discussing the exam with Murray and at the same time vaguely wondering about Dr Brown when the latter noticed him, smiled and slid off his bar stool to come along and join them.

'Dr Brown . . . Charles Murray. Up for the exam. Charles . . .'

'Of course . . . And you too, David. How did it go?'

Campbell and Murray each waited for the other to answer the question. There was a pause. Dr Brown smiled and said, 'We never got round to our chat about neurology for the examiners, did we, David? I hope you still did yourself credit on anything that came up.'

'There was one case . . .' Campbell outlined the story of the middle-aged woman.

'Hm,' said Dr Brown. 'I doubt if that case was submitted by a real neurologist . . . But you can see what they're getting at. The general feel of it is something in the subacute sclerosing panencephalitis line, with just a whiff of something very nasty in the way of a malignancy. A real horrendoma. Five days of symptoms, hm? Well, they're certainly asking you to think along these sorts of lines. Don't tell me you thought it was a bleed, David.'

'It didn't sound like one.'

'What did you think of it, Charles?'

'Didn't try that one, sir. Not clever enough. There was an old thing with a sore shoulder who looked a lot easier. Of course, I could have been way off beam . . .'

They discussed the old lady again, then the lorry driver. Murray seemed fairly impressed by the neurologist's view on a gastrointestinal problem, and said so, then excused himself in order to get to Waverley in time for his London train. As soon as he had left Dr Brown reached into his pocket. 'You'll probably feel like another, David. Exams always gave me a terrible thirst. Gin and tonic?'

'Thanks.'

Dr Brown stood waiting to catch the barmaid's eye. Campbell decided that he had most probably not been lurking for a dubious assignation, or in the process of drinking himself to a solitary death. He was probably just lonely. He had, Campbell realized, talked a lot about himself, but never about his home or family. Perhaps he would this evening, or perhaps he never would. Meanwhile, a chance had arisen to catch up with one or two things about work with one who, in normal working hours, had proved more than ordinarily elusive.

'Thank you, Dr Brown.'

'Cheers. What about the data interpretation, David? How did that go. Usually it's the kind of stuff you either know or you don't.'

'Well, I didn't know much of it. But the slides could have been worse, I suppose. Maybe about a third of them were . . .'

'Any neurology?'

'A girl with a birthmark on her right cheek.'

'Ah. Our old friend trigeminal neurangiomatosis.'

'Good. That's what I said it was.'

Although Campbell was beginning to get bored by further discussion of what might turn out to be a regrettable occasion, Dr Brown seemed to be enjoying the game, so to speak, from the trainer's bench, and talked confidently and, so far as Campbell could judge, competently about the various possibilities the questions evoked. It took some time for conversation to revert to the affairs of the Unit. Campbell raised a general point about data storage and processing, prompted by his bizarre encounter with Dr Frank, though not mentioning her by name.

'Ah, big advances there, David. At long last. I've been pushing Hamburg to give us a lot more backup on that one. After all, more or less half the evaluation patients in the whole trial are in Edinburgh. And at last they've decided to do something. I shouldn't complain, they've really been remarkably generous over most things. You can't run an international multicentre drug evaluation trial on a shoestring, but in data management they have skimped a bit, so far. I think, because we really have a trial that's outstripped its original data-handling provision. But that's all changing, as indeed it should.'

'What's going to happen?'

'Well, a couple of heavies are due over from Germany next week to discuss things. So I think we can anticipate a major overhaul. They're very much in the business of helping us, of course, and everyone concerned – Dr Robson, yourself, and me – will be involved in the discussions. I suppose we could go out to lunch somewhere. Maybe the Howtowdie . . . or Cousteau's.'

Campbell sipped his drink and thought about that. One major omission might be worth mentioning. 'What about . . . existing arrangements? I mean Dr Frank.'

Dr Brown paused and looked very thoughtful, then shook his head. 'The strain . . . I think the strain was too much for her. It was a colossal job for one person. She's actually back in hospital now. Perhaps for some time. I should have spotted the trouble earlier, but you know how busy I've been. This Aix-en-Provence business was just the last straw.'

'Hospital?'

'Morningside.'

The district of Morningside harboured what Campbell liked to think of as a complex of psychiatric institutions. 'Really? What was the trouble?'

'Strain . . . on a brilliant mind. You didn't really know her, did you?'

'Not really.'

'Terribly intense girl. Conscientious to a fault, and always had her troubles. You must have noticed that yourself, David, in people with exceptional mathematical gifts.'

'Is she depressed?'

'That's putting it rather strongly. But yes.'

Had Campbell been invited to pass a clinical opinion on the haggard and haunted woman who had shuffled past him in the Neurobiology Unit he would have said schizophrenic, on treatment, with side-effects. Depression might be a characteristically Brownian euphemism. Campbell murmured something polite about their colleague's illness. Dr Brown said that her going into hospital was probably for the best, as she had evidently benefited enormously on a previous occasion. There was a silence, which Campbell eventually ended by offering to buy Dr Brown a drink.

'Thanks, yes. But I'll have to rush off fairly shortly. One of those supper colloquia. To tell you the truth, I'd as soon give it a miss, but you know how it is. People expect you. Ah, thanks. And how are the new referrals coming along? I'd hoped to see a few myself, but you know how it's been.'

'Well, the new referrals have sort of levelled off, but the follow-up clinic's been getting quite busy.'

'That makes it all the more important to get this data-handling business sorted out once and for all. How did you get on with old McVittie.'

'Hm. Funny old chap. How old is he?'

'Oh, seventy-five. Maybe seventy-six.'

'He talked about how things were in nineteen forty-eight.'

'He usually does. But he's going to keep sending us cases?'

'Well, he knows about the Unit.'

'Good, good. Thanks, David. People really do need reminding. And this is such a terribly important study. The first thing there's been for dementia that actually works.' Dr Brown gazed into his fresh drink. 'We've actually got something that works . . . The French are just as keen on it as we are. Old Boigny, with his two dozen patients . . . He's most impressed with it. What I had to do last week was go down there and ask why, if he's so impressed with it, hasn't he found another hundred patients.' Dr Brown livened to a little bit of Gallic shrugging. ' "But my dear Dr Brown, our little clinique is not your great beeg Edimbourg . . ." The old rogue probably makes more money letting the patients lie around all day in his famous medicinal mud baths. You know, David, sometimes I find myself agreeing with whoever it was who said that abroad was bloody and foreigners simply frightful. But I suppose we have a duty to science . . . And at least they're more or less organized in Tijuana.'

Campbell, wondering if this might be a preamble to the announcement of yet another international excursion, asked how things were in Tijuana.

'The dements are Mexican, and there are quite a few of

them. I think fifty at the last count. But the know-how is American, thank God. Roomfuls of psychology PhDs with tight jeans and a sort of . . . earnest loveliness. You'll probably come across one or two of them at the Eastern Mediterranean Conference. Bright girls, some of them. We advertised for Spanish-speaking psychology majors and just interviewed the first fifty with PhDs. It's quite a setup. So the way things are going, we'll all be quite famous by the end of October.'

There was another longish pause, and Campbell remembered an aspect of the Unit's work that had been causing him continuing disquiet. Eventually he found a tactful way of putting it. 'There don't appear to have been any more deaths.'

'Deaths, David?'

'Deaths on treatment. With Auragen.'

'It's pretty safe stuff.'

'The other day I was trying to find out what dose the follow-up lady had been taking.'

'You couldn't, without access to the code.'

'So I gathered. But the old lady in the ward . . . Mrs Spence. She'd just started on the bigger dose.'

'Come on, David. A woman of ninety-six with advanced coronary artery disease . . . As the PM showed. As I said, we take note of these things.'

'I thought I'd better notify them as well. You know. To the Committee on the Safety of Medicines.'

'You haven't, David . . .'

'No, but I thought I probably should.'

'No need, David.'

'But if they're on a new drug . . .'

'No need, David. I notified CSM myself about both of them, as soon as you told me. Safety is a number one consideration in this trial . . . Simply because we're dealing with such a vulnerable population. So not to worry, David. It's all been seen to . . . Goodness, is that the time? Well. Duty calls. And I do hope all's well with the membership. A sensible chap like yourself should encounter no particular problems with the examiners. Good night.'

*   *   *

'Sister was ever so cross. "How can I run a ward if that man . . ." – That's what she calls him, "that man" – "How can I run a ward if that man pops in an average of three times a week about half past three in the afternoon sucking a Polo mint and saying, 'Sister, I've got another delightful old lady who'll greatly benefit from a week or so in your tender care . . .'?" And you know how it is, David. Usually they're horrible.'

Dr Phillips shook some salad out onto a paper plate and attacked a cold half chicken with a knife borrowed from the residency pantry. 'I don't think the other consultants like him either. Dr Temple's always very polite, but you can tell. They call each other Dr Temple and Dr Brown and hardly ever speak anyway. I think the other two hope he'll go away.'

'Probably.'

'If you imagine the wards without him you can see why.'

'I suppose Barry likes it the way it is. He's got lots of scope.'

'Barry won't stay long.'

'Oh?'

'He wants to rotate out to rheumatology. Is that enough chicken?'

'Thanks, Jo.'

With a small unsteady corkscrew Campbell broached a bottle of hock, uncertain of any style or impressiveness in the matter, but fairly sure that Jo wouldn't mind if he ended up simply smashing the neck off on a rock. That proved unnecessary. He poured two fairish measures into paper cups.

'Cheers.'

'Cheers.'

'It didn't rain.'

'It hasn't yet.'

Jo laughed, and they ate their picnic, half sheltered by the Scimitar, on a sunny, blowy headland looking out across a bay to the open sea. Later, over some very ripe Stilton, they discussed Bobby again.

'D'you think he'll get the chair, David?'

'I don't know. I think he thinks he will. But he's worried. He keeps talking about somebody called Sinclair who's in

London just now but wants to come back. I don't know much about him.'

'Barry says he's very bright but a bit common for a neurologist.'

'Well, he should know.'

'David . . .'

'I think Bobby thinks that the Auragen results will clinch it for him.'

'Will they?'

'I doubt it. It's up to the committee, and what the stuff looks like when it's published. But I'm not so sure. People who're keen on it are so keen on it they've sort of lost track of whether it works or not. It's as if they're selling the stuff rather than evaluating it. Hell, maybe they are. You know that Kristall Morgen paid for the Unit.'

'Salaries for all those funny research people?'

'Hmmm. Yes. That as well. But they actually coughed up a hundred thousand to build it in the first place.'

'Did they?'

'So I suppose they want some results for their money. It's all very messy. Two people are coming across from Hamburg this week.'

Jo pointed the residency table knife at Campbell and said, 'We have ways of making you produce results.'

'As far as I know, they'll just be taking us out to lunch.'

'All these drug companies are the same.' Jo buttered another biscuit and handed it to Campbell. 'We had one that more or less took over a coronary care unit in Manchester. They had this stuff that made you very strange and sick. The ECG tracings looked a lot better though. Then it was withdrawn.'

'Why? Did it kill people?'

'I think most of them were dying anyway. No, it was just another flavour-of-the-month wonder drug, not much different from all the others. And some of the others didn't make you as sick.'

'Auragen's probably just that. A flavour-of-the-month wonder drug, but with big money behind it. I'm getting a bit fed up with it. Asking people all those silly questions.'

114

'And having Bobby bouncing around breathing over you.'

'That as well. If I pass I'll get out. If I don't, I don't know. Maybe hang around for another shot. Jobs are so tight in the medical specialties. Have you got anything fixed up?'

'A year doing sex therapy. Then obs and gynae.'

'Really? Sex therapy?'

'I don't tell many people. They get the wrong idea. But I thought it would be all right for you to know. Now.'

Campbell topped up their paper cups. A seagull drifted past sideways, eyeing the last of the Stilton.

The following Saturday, in a bookshop in the New Town, Campbell met a doctor, a few years older than himself, whom he had known for years. Neil Aytoun had been the senior registrar in a medical unit where Campbell had done time as a student, and had then been a quiet, amusing and effective junior hospital doctor. He had subsequently disappeared to the USA for a couple of years, to escape, it was alleged, the attentions of the downstairs ward sister, but had more recently returned to a local consultancy in diabetes. Early in their acquaintance he had seemed to Campbell an ordinary young teaching-hospital man, innocent of redeeming eccentricities, but at the unit's beer and skittles night he had revealed himself as a jazz pianist of note, even when drunk. He stood now, browsing among recent nonfiction. Campbell, not too engrossed in a large book about an unimportant spy, returned his nod of recognition. Dr Aytoun came across to talk, still carrying a TV announcer's memoirs.

'How are things, David?'

'All right. And you?'

'Can't afford books any more.'

Dr Aytoun, slight and dapper and now greying a little round the temples, sporting a collar and tie even on a Saturday, seemed to have come a long way from the skittle alley and the piano with three pints of beer waiting on top.

'Back at the Institute?'

'For a while anyway. Having a go at membership.'

'This time?'

'Yes.'

'Clinicals next week?'

'That's right.'

'Where?'

'Leith.'

'Really?' Dr Aytoun seemed quite interested. 'Tuesday or Wednesday?'

'Wednesday.'

'Well, we might meet.'

'Oh?'

'I'm examining at Leith on Wednesday.'

'Really?'

'Yes. Wednesday's clinicals. We might meet. Are you all ready?'

'As ready as I'm going to be. A last session of the Sunday school at the Southern tomorrow, and that's it. Take my chance.'

'First time?'

'Yes.'

Dr Aytoun hesitated, then smiled and said, 'Mine too. So make allowances. Examiners get nerves too, you know. But best of luck.'

'And you.'

He smiled a twinkly smile and was gone, still carrying the announcer's memoirs. Campbell put down the spy book and savoured the prospect of being examined at Leith, on pendular nystagmus, for example, by Neil Aytoun. The coincidence, and knowing who one of his examiners would be, was not disagreeable, but seemed to bring Wednesday quite a lot closer.

Next day, at the Sunday school, one of Bertram's consultant colleagues tore Campbell to pieces over a straightforward case of cirrhosis, grilled him for twelve minutes on the eye signs in thyrotoxicosis, showed him four impossible skin rashes about which he could talk in general terms only, then tried to cheer him up over coffee.

'It all depends on how things go on the day. I mean, you're not usually as bad as that. I was examining the last time round. It's conceivable you would have passed.'

'Really?'

116

'Yes.' Campbell's last pre-membership clinical teacher nodded and sipped his coffee. 'Standards are dropping all the time.'

'It's hard to explain . . . I just didn't feel well. So it didn't really start at any particular time. I'd go to a match – a football match – and come home just not feeling right. Not ill. Just not right.'

'Tired?'

'I suppose so. But not like tired after your work. Just no energy.'

'And you went to your doctor?'

'Well, I put it off, to tell you the truth. You don't go to the doctor and say your feeling tired. But it got worse.'

'Until?'

'Until she made me go.'

'And then?'

'I got a tonic. A sort of pick-me-up, he said.'

'Did that help?'

'No. So the second time he gave me a cough bottle.'

'You had a cough?'

'Just a wee dry tickle.'

'Did the bottle help?'

'No.'

'Tell me about the cough.'

'Well . . . a cough. Just a cough. Ordinary.'

'Did you bring anything up?'

'No. It was a dry cough.'

'No phlegm?'

'No.'

'No blood?'

'No.'

'Worse in the mornings?'

'Maybe.' The man smiled patiently. 'Coughs usually are.'

'Do you smoke, Mr Hurst?'

'No . . . It's a mug's game.'

'Did you ever smoke?'

'Used to. Gave it up. It's a mug's game.'

117

'Have you ever had any chest trouble before, Mr Hurst?'

'Have I got chest trouble now?'

'Well, you've got a cough. How about other things? Your appetite?'

'Not so good.'

'Your weight?'

'Sort of steady.'

'Sort of?'

'Well, maybe a wee bit down.'

'Any pain in your chest?'

'No.'

'Breathlessness.'

'Well, maybe running for a bus.'

'Wheeze?'

'No. I never wheeze.'

'And your general health?'

'All right. Always been very good, until this tired feeling.'

'Do you get indigestion?'

'Not really . . . No.'

'Heartburn?'

'Sometimes.'

'Discomfort? Fullness after meals?'

'Well, maybe a bit. Depends what I eat.'

'Anything that disagrees with you?'

'Well . . . big meals, maybe. Enough's enough for me.'

'Sickness?'

'Being sick?'

'Or just feeling sick?'

'Not really.'

'Not really?'

'Just sometimes. Maybe after big meals.'

'Bowels all right?'

'Fine.'

'Not constipated.'

'No. More the other way.'

'Blood? Or bowels movements a funny colour? Dark?'

'Nothing like that.'

'Ever get pain after food?'

'Well . . . no. Not as a regular thing.'

'But sometimes.'

'Sometimes.'

'After any particular food?'

'No . . . But maybe after a big meal. A few hours later.'

'Ever get pain at night? Like indigestion?'

'Funny you should mention that. Yes. Sometimes. There . . .'

'What do you take for that?'

'You mean a bottle or something?'

'Anything.'

'Milk. But I never got a bottle. From the doctor, I mean.'

'How long have you been getting it? The pain at night?'

'Months . . . But I never mentioned it to the doctor. So I never got a bottle. Milk helps a bit. And I tried her indigestion bottle once.'

'Did it help?'

'A bit.'

'But you never mentioned it to your own doctor?'

'He never asked questions like you.' The man smiled and so did Campbell.

'I'm sorry about all this. Nearly finished. Then I want to examine you.'

'Go right ahead, doc.'

Mr Hurst was sixty-one, married, with two grown-up children. He worked in a paper mill in a small town just out of Edinburgh, he had been in hospital for about a week with a story that did not, so far at least, add up to anything in particular, and he was Campbell's long case in membership. He was a concise and sensible witness of events. Campbell, seated at his bedside, scribbled a few more notes about his inquiries.

'I'm sorry,' said Mr Hurst. 'If I knew what was wrong I would tell you.'

'Don't apologize,' said Campbell. 'I think I'm supposed to find out for myself, anyway.' A useful thought occurred. 'What tests have you had?'

'Since I came in?'

'Yes.'

'Well, they took a lot of blood.'

'Yes?'

'Then some more.'

'Oh. And X-rays? Anything like that?'

'Oh yes. My chest. And a barium meal.'

'Oh. A lot of chest X-rays?'

'One from the back and a couple from the side.'

'Thanks, Mr Hurst. What was your health like before all this started?'

'Fine. Played football – at the works, you know – till I was fifty. This is the first time I've been in hospital, apart from glandular fever in the army.'

'On any tablets or medicine?'

'The cough bottle.'

'Do you drink?'

'Weddings and funerals. And New Year, of course.'

'Of course. And you gave up smoking?'

'Yes. A while ago.'

Campbell asked a few more routine questions, then began to examine Mr Hurst, starting at his hands then moving to head and neck, chest and abdomen, and finishing with a quick look at the central nervous system which, given the story, was unlikely to contribute much.

As he worked he thought about the case and, prompted by the near absence of physical signs, remembered a few more things he ought to have asked about: night sweats in keeping with TB; possible contact with infectious chest disease; anything in the previous or family history to support the diagnosis of duodenal ulcer.

Physical examination proved almost entirely unhelpful. Mr Hurst looked quite fit for his age. If he had lost weight he had not lost much. He was a little pale. Campbell was disconcerted to find nothing in the examination of the chest to go with the story of the cough. Mr Hurst was minimally tender when Campbell pressed him in the place where duodenal ulcers usually hurt most, and that was all.

'Well, doc?'

'Anyone in the family have ulcer trouble?'

'My father. Terrible ulcers. Had the operation and they came back.'

120

'And I wondered if anyone you know, anyone at work, or at home, had chest trouble recently.'

'Not that I know of.'

'And have you noticed yourself sweating more, at night?'

'No . . . I don't think so.'

'Thanks, Mr Hurst. Could I just go over your chest again? And maybe your neck . . .'

Once more there was nothing to find: no area of dullness or altered breath sounds to confirm malignant or other consolidation, and no lumps in the neck which would have denoted a spreading cancer, most probably originating in the lung.

Someone, probably Bertram, had once given Campbell some general advice about diagnosis: uncommon presentations of common things were more common than uncommon things. The ulcer was straightforward enough: the family history, the night pain and the characteristically localized tenderness made the diagnosis. The chest problem was less straightforward: the cough and the smoking history, together with the probably related recent malaise, were, on the basis that common things happen commonly, probably indicative of a lung tumour, though other illnesses could account for all three features.

Something a little more diagnostic, such as blood in the sputum, typical alterations in the fingertips or the presence of affected lymph nodes in the neck, would, from Campbell's point of view, have been welcome, but what he had would do quite well as a somewhat less than typical presentation of a common disease, so it remained the best bet. And there was no possibility, or at least none that occurred to Campbell, which would tie up what had appeared to be two separate sets of symptoms in one neat diagnostic compartment. No. Common things happened commonly, and lots of people had two common diseases. But then again, this was the clinical examination for membership of the Royal College of Physicians of Edinburgh, so perhaps a rare syndrome, a neat subsuming single answer which had yet evaded Campbell was on offer.

'I think it's an ulcer myself,' said Mr Hurst. 'My dad used to get up and drink milk in the middle of the night too.'

Campbell gathered up his notes, stethoscope and tendon

hammer. 'Thanks, Mr Hurst. I think we might be back. You know, with the examiners.'

'Best of luck, doc.'

'Thanks, Mr Hurst.'

There were ten minutes left in which to put things together and go back, if necessary, to check over a point from the history or the physical findings. Campbell sat on the uncomfortable chair provided and scribbled down a few main points to stop himself getting sidetracked into the unimportant or the unlikely. 'Man in 60s. Ex-smoker. Unproductive cough. Slight wt loss.' And on top of all that, whatever it was, there was a fairly ordinary-sounding DU. Unfortunately for Mr Hurst, the likeliest chest diagnosis was lung cancer, with tubercle a poor second and whole lot of less likely things running third to a hundred and fiftieth or whatever. Industrial chest disease: unlikely. Atypical pneumonia: maybe. And so on, from aspergillosis to Zenker's oesophageal diverticulum, which was said to present some-times with a cough, though usually one that was worse at night.

At least the business of preparing a short and coherent account of a case was one that Campbell had practised every Sunday morning for six weeks. Bertram and his colleagues had made much of this, encouraging the good and pouring scorn on minor lapses. ('One more negative finding and I'll scream.' 'Boring. They fail bores, you know.') Five minutes hurried but routine work sorted out the story of who Mr Hurst was and what had happened to him. Then came the difficult bit. Campbell wrote down '1. DU' then '2. Ca bronchus *or* tubercle *or* (pos-sibly) atypical pneumonia'. He had just turned his mind to the series of tests which would sort out the various possibilities into one firm respiratory diagnosis when the registrar who had introduced him to Mr Hurst an hour before came back and said, 'Time, please, Dr Campbell. Would you like to come this way?'

The two examiners sat in a bleak little room of the sort generally used for imparting bad news to patients' relatives. Neither was Dr Aytoun. Campbell knew one of them by sight: a thin and reputedly stupid little woman with an interest in diabetes; the other, a tall, stout man, was unfamiliar, probably not from Edinburgh. The woman spoke first. 'Good morning, Dr Hurst.'

Although the general wisdom on passing membership ran against arguing with the examiners, Campbell felt he could not let this pass. He coughed and said, 'Campbell. I'm Dr Campbell.'

The woman peered angrily at him, then looked down and shuffled the papers on her knee. 'You've been *seeing* Mr Hurst, I mean. Obviously. I'm Dr Humphreys. And this is Dr Bland. You, I take it, are Dr Campbell.'

'Yes.'

'Good morning.'

'Good morning.'

The large man smiled at Campbell but did not say anything.

'Tell us, please, about Mr Hurst, Dr Campbell,' said Dr Humphreys. 'In your own words.'

'You haven't mentioned diabetes . . .' The woman was looking angry again. Dr Bland, her co-examiner, clutched his brow, causing Campbell to wonder how many previous candidates might have thus been challenged already that morning.

'The family history was negative. And nothing in Mr Hurst's symptoms . . .'

'What about his weight loss?'

'Well . . . the routine urinalysis and blood sugar . . .'

'You didn't mention that.'

'No.'

'And can you tell me what percentage of new diabetics have no family history of the disease?'

From the air, or from a half-forgotten textbook, Campbell clutched a figure. 'Twenty-five per cent.'

Dr Humphreys pursed her lips. 'It's actually twenty-seven. That's several hundred thousand diabetics in the United Kingdom. And his anorexia is highly suggestive too. Neglect diabetes at your peril, Dr Hurst.'

Dr Bland had ceased to clutch his brow and was now

pinching the bridge of his nose tightly between the thumb and forefinger of his right hand. Dr Humphreys appeared to have no more questions. Dr Bland opened his eyes, let go of the bridge of his nose and spoke for the first time. 'Moving on from the very important topic of diabetes, Dr Campbell . . . what did you think was actually wrong with this patient?'

'As I said, he's got a duodenal ulcer, on the history and examination. And as well as that he's got weight loss, malaise and an unproductive cough, with no related signs that I could find on examination. So he certainly needs a chest X-ray, with a bronchogenic carcinoma high on the list of possibilities . . .'

'And the rest of your list?'

'Well, tubercle's less common in this age group now than it was, but it needs to be excluded. I wondered about atypical pneumonia. And possibly fibrosing alveolitis, but I would have expected more in the way of breathlessness.'

'So you're telling me he's got a bronchogenic?'

'It's high on the list. First, in fact.'

Dr Bland smiled. 'You're putting your money on lung cancer?'

Campbell nodded. The examiner's accent was unfamiliar and vaguely menacing. 'That's the most likely thing.'

'No blood in his spit?'

'No.'

'No finger clubbing?'

'No.'

'No glands in his neck?'

'No.'

'So what's the next step?'

'Chest X-ray. And probably a lateral too.'

'Then?'

'Sputum for cytology, looking for malignant cells. Then bronchoscopy.'

'If I told you now that he'd had all those things, and there's no evidence of a bronchogenic carcinoma . . .?'

Campbell was taken aback. A bronchoscopy, which involved a general anaesthetic, a lot of messing about with tubes and a sore throat when you woke up, was something Mr

124

Hurst really ought to have mentioned. Or perhaps, since it was so thoroughly unpleasant, he had genuinely forgotten it. 'I see.'

'So he's got a cough, and some weight loss, a normal chest X-ray and nothing on bronchoscopy to suggest lung cancer. Did you examine his abdomen, Dr Campbell?'

'Yes.'

'Find anything abnormal?'

'Epigastric tenderness. In keeping with a DU.'

'And?'

Campbell sat silently. He had missed something important.

'Perhaps, Dr Campbell, we should go back and take another look . . .' He pronounced it 'luck'. At least the mystery of the examiner's accent was solved: by association with breathless, on-the-spot TV accounts of bombings, knee-cappings and murders, the mild and persistent Dr Bland, with his clipped and half-swallowed vowels, probably came from Belfast.

Mr Hurst lay as requested, flat on his back with his pyjama jacket and trousers undone.

'Muster Hurst, Dr Campbell here would like to examine your abdomen again . . .'

Campbell knelt by the bed in the approved manner, as done only in exams. Mr Hurst was nicely relaxed. Campbell, knowing he had missed something, and looking for it now under the critical gaze of the examiners, was not. His mouth was dry and his hand shook as he laid it gently on the pale skin of Mr Hurst's belly. He was looking for the answer to a kind of diagnostic crossword-puzzle clue: easily missed abdominal abnormality accounting for something that looks like lung cancer but isn't. He felt his way softly, from top left to top right to bottom right and bottom left of the abdomen, which is what you did in exams, then more firmly in the top left, under the ribs. There was a vague suspicion of resistance, nothing more.

'Well, Dr Campbell?'

'I'd like to feel for his spleen.'

'Carry on.'

There was ritual for that too. You made the patient lie

leaning to the right, and felt with both hands, one behind the left ribs, the other under them, preferably maintaining a calm exterior throughout.

'Well?'

'Thanks, Mr Hurst.' Campbell stood up and faced the examiners. 'He's got a slightly enlarged spleen.'

'Fine. Let's go somewhere quiet and talk about that.'

The accent remained vaguely menacing. Campbell followed the large man, feeling rather as if he were being taken to an interrogation centre to assist in RUC inquiries into the causes of an enlarged spleen and his reasons for failing to find it. They returned to the little room and sat down again. Big spleens and weight loss were nasty. The cough remained unaccounted for. The man from Belfast was very determined.

Ten minutes later Campbell emerged, pale and sweating. Dr Humphreys had sat silent while Dr Bland had grilled Campbell on weight loss and big spleens and how you investigated the combination. Like a good interrogator he had extracted things his victim hadn't even known he'd known. The big question, however, remained unanswered. For several weeks afterwards Campbell had nightmares in which a relentless Ulsterman asked, 'And how do you account for the cough? You can't explain it? Now think again . . . It's very important and you probably know the answer. Why has Muster Hurst got a cough?'

At the end, when they let him go, Campbell stood outside the little room wondering where he would sit the exam next time. From nowhere, the registrar appeared again and led him to another ward and another batch of inquisitors: two men standing in dark suits in the middle of a circle of variously disrobed patients in beds and chairs. The taller was one Dr Liddle, a gloomy and exacting endocrinologist unpopular with students and probably not the sort of chap you would pick to examine you in membership if you had a choice. The other was Neil Aytoun.

Campbell walked towards them, stopped at a respectful distance, said, 'Good morning,' and smiled in the direction of Dr Aytoun. Dr Aytoun did not smile back. Indeed, both examiners wore expressions of faintly hostile solemnity, like judges agreeing that twenty-five years would be about right. There was a long moment of unease, then the senior examiner, in a curious, strangled nasal tone that Campbell had heard imitated more often than he had heard it at first hand, said, 'Good morning, Dr Campbell. I'd like you to examine Mrs Patie's ocular control.'

They moved towards the patient indicated, and as they did so Campbell could see that her eyes were wobbling regularly and quite fast in the horizontal plane: she had the pendular nystagmus Bones had warned him about. He held a finger up in front of her nose, asked her to look at it and raised it slowly to the upper limit of her field of vision. Campbell, who had never seen a case before, was gratified to see that the wobble increased in amplitude, exactly as the textbook had said it would. Perhaps his luck was turning.

'Well, Dr Campbell?'

'Thank you, Mrs Patie. Well, sir, she's got pendular nystagmus.'

'A condition associated with . . .?'

'Retinal disorders involving loss of central vision.'

'And . . .?'

'Occasionally in multiple sclerosis.'

'Does Mrs Patie have multiple sclerosis? Quickly, Dr Campbell.'

Campbell held his finger up in front of the patient again and asked her to touch it, first with her right index finger, then with her left. She did this quickly and precisely, without any suggestion of unsteadiness. 'Probably not.'

'Yes or no?'

'No.'

Silent and expressionless, the examiners had walked on and stopped beside a seated middle-aged man. 'Hands,' said Dr Liddle.

The man had little excrescences arising from the nailfolds and affecting most of his fingers.

'Well?'

'Um . . .'

'Well?'

'Um . . . warts.' Campbell waited for some reaction from

either of the examiners. There was none. They had walked on again and were standing on either side of a woman who looked as if she'd had a stroke. 'Test for sensory involvement,' said Dr Liddle, mainly through his nose.

Campbell knelt in front of the woman and asked her to close her eyes and then say where he was touching her. She could feel even the lightest touch on both hands, but there was sometimes a more subtle loss, and Campbell tested for that by touching her on the back of both hands at the same time and asking which side he had touched. She hesitated, then said, 'The right.'

'She's got extinction of light touch on the left.'

'Yes?'

Extinction of light touch on the left was clearly not enough. Campbell glanced up at his examiners. Both stared sullenly down. Campbell remembered something else that sometimes went wrong and asked the woman to grasp her left thumb with her right hand, first with her eyes open, then with them closed. Eyes closed, she groped hopelessly. She had lost position sense as well. 'Her proprioception's been affected too.'

The examiners had begun to move on. Campbell got up and followed them. They stopped by a young man lying on his bed with his pyjama jacket open. 'Auscultate the precordium, Dr Campbell.'

Most people would have simply said listen to his heart. Campbell got his stethoscope out and before actually listening went through another of the little rituals by laying a hand flat over the patient's heart, a much venerated but rarely rewarded manoeuvre that occasionally picked up angross abnormality of the valves. 'I said listen, Dr Campbell. Just listen.'

Campbell listened without hope. Abnormal heart sounds, other than the most obvious, had never meant much to him, and membership murmurs were known to be difficult if not frankly inaudible to non-experts. Among the various soft and probably normal thumps was a very soft and intermittent swish that might or might not mean a narrowing of one particular valve. Campbell listened as long as he dared then straightened up and took his stethoscope out of his ears.

'Well?'.

Though he had been given no feedback whatsoever, either verbal or visual, Campbell had an impression that short answers might be preferred, so he said, 'Normal heart sounds, and a soft systolic murmur. Probably pulmonary.'

Dr Liddle remained as impassive as ever. Dr Aytoun, having glanced sideways at his senior colleague, did so too. It was all very puzzling. Campbell began to wonder what would happen if he said something that he knew was wildly wrong or inappropriate. ('No idea. Sounds like a tap-dancer with asthma in there. I really haven't a clue. Thank you and good morning.') Dr Liddle and Dr Aytoun exchanged expressionless gazes and moved on, then, as though by some prearranged signal, Dr Liddle stood back and Dr Aytoun, more sullen and impassive than Campbell would have believed possible, showed him five more cases. Two Campbell was reasonably sure about, one was doubtful but worth a guess, and the remaining two, a retina and a curious ring-shaped rash, simply hopeless. They reached the end of the semicircle and Campbell was dismissed with a nasal 'Good morning'.

So finished his clinical exam. He had missed a spleen in his long case, and performed somewhere between very and moderately badly in the short cases. The last part of the exam, a viva voce with yet another pair of examiners at the college in the afternoon, did not count for much towards the total and, in any case, the rules were clear that if you had failed at the bedside no amount of brilliance across the table could retrieve your fortunes. Campbell left the hospital by a side door and walked down to where his car was parked, vaguely hoping that no one he knew would see him.

After the longest morning Campbell could remember it was only half past eleven. He sat in his car and watched two swans, pristine in a grubby backwater of the harbour, spread their wings and drift away before the breeze. The spleen, and his failure to find it, were now in the regrettable, irretrievable past. It had not even been a particularly difficult spleen to feel, and there was no excuse for his not having found it on his own, in the first hour of the exam and without prompting. But it had been there and he had missed it and that was almost certainly the end of his hopes of a first-time pass and an early escape from the Neurobiology job. Having heard how-I-failed-membership stories since he was a fourth-year medical student, Campbell found himself beginning to work on his own. The examiner's Ulster accent would probably come into it, as might the patient's culpable failure to report the bronchoscopy, though it was true that without also being informed of the result he would have been no further forward.

Three hours remained before the final round in this attempt at membership. There was absolutely no point in reading any more. With the whole of medicine to choose from, the examiners could ask about anything from acne to schizophrenia, and good luck to them. If he could assist with their inquiries, he would; if he could not, he would not bluff, but follow Bertram's advice ('Honest confession, good for the soul') and hope they might move on to something less unpromising. Meanwhile there were three hours to pass somehow, then another twenty-four or so before the results went up and all hope vanished.

Down in the harbour, a ship's siren sounded three blasts. Campbell started his car and drove back to the Institute by the scenic route, taking an agreeable detour round Arthur's Seat and thinking about things other than those which the examiners might wish to discuss in the afternoon.

At the reception desk in the Neurobiology Unit Fiona stopped typing when Campbell came in and told him he was looking awfully smart and that someone from London had called and could he call back. The message slip read 'Mr Baxter (Omar): ring back this a.m., please', and gave a London number that was becoming familiar.

'Thanks, Fiona.'

'Are you trying to escape?'

'Hm?'

'The suit. Sneaking off for an interview somewhere?'

'Oh, no. No. An exam. Membership, actually.'

'This afternoon?'

'This morning as well.'

'Go all right?'

'No.'

'Oh, well. Maybe you'll make up for it this afternoon.'

'Thanks, Fiona.'

Campbell went to his office and rang the Office of Medical Appointments (Reserves) immediately, and asked to speak to Chief Backstay. A polite and apologetic rating informed Campbell that the CPOMA had gone down to his mess and would thereafter be taking a make and mend, so could sir ring back in the morning, preferably around stand easy. Much refreshed by an earful of naval jargon, sir said, 'Roger,' thanked the LMA and hung up wondering whether, if the chief had offered him a nice jolly in the Windies or the Far Flung, he could have refused.

Still ruminating on the minor disgrace of failing a first attempt at membership, Campbell went alone to lunch in the Institute's dining room. As he moved into the servery and paused to read the menu a short fat middle-aged physio-therapist waddled past him, cutting ahead of him in the queue and knocking his tray from his hand. She turned in perfunc-tory apology and was much taken aback when Campbell, still morose and preoccupied by the morning's struggle, glared at her and called her a clumsy cow. She bit her lip, blushed and sniffed and did not fully regain her composure until she had taken delivery of a crowded plate of steak and kidney pudding and chips. Stuck immediately behind her, Campbell followed her through as far as the cash register, uncomfortably aware of her colleagues behind him, and embarrassed and repentant about his reaction to her really rather pathetic haste in the matter of lunch. With liver and onions and a small salad on his tray he eventually escaped his victim and, conscious of having compounded his academic failure by a major social lapse, headed shamefacedly for the farthest and quietest corner of the dining room.

At an empty and secluded table he put down his lunch and

131

went off to dispose of his tray and find a water jug and a glass. When he returned there was someone else at the table. He had been joined by a familiar, grey, stooping presence: Dr H. J. S. Creech MD, FRCPE, a very senior physician and his old medical chief. Fussy and lugubrious, Creech unloaded a tray of brown windsor soup, steak and kidney pudding with sprouts and boiled potatoes, and a plate of rather solid-looking apple crumble and custard.

'I hope you don't mind me joining you.'

'Not at all, sir.'

Campbell took Creech's tray and went to fetch another glass. Creech poured water for both, then said, 'Is there something bothering you?'

'Bothering me, sir?'

'Yes . . . You really weren't very nice to that silly woman in the queue. Not like you. So is there something bothering you?'

Campbell sighed. Creech sat with his spoon poised over his soup, waiting for details.

'I think I've failed membership.'

'Really?'

'So . . . when that woman . . .'

'Yes . . . I saw that. But what about membership? Clinicals today?'

'This morning.'

'And orals this afternoon?'

'Yes.'

'And you think you've failed.'

'Pretty-sure. Missed a spleen in my long case.'

Creech took a noisy mouthful of soup. 'But nobody's failed until the exam's over.'

'I suppose not.'

'And when I've been examining I've passed people who've missed spleens. Obviously not if you can see it from the end of the bed. But clinical technique's only part of it. You could still pass. How did the short cases go?'

'Not very well.'

'How many did they show you?'

'Nine, I think.'

132

'Well, you can't have been doing too badly. They don't show you a whole lot if you're really struggling. So don't give up. Just go along to the oral and do your best, and forget all about that spleen. You haven't failed until the list goes up and your name's not on it . . . I wondered about the liver myself.'

'The liver, sir?'

'Yes. What you're having. But the steak and kidney's usually pretty good . . . No, you shouldn't give up. Just go down there and give a reasonable account of yourself in the oral, and then forget about the whole thing till the list goes up tomorrow.'

Campbell ate slowly, partly because he wasn't hungry, partly because he had two courses fewer than his senior companion. Creech stopped talking and polished off his soup, putting his plate to one side and reaching happily for his steak and kidney pudding.

'When are you due down at the college?'

'Half past two.'

'That's good. Have a look at the *BMJ* because all the examiners do. And give yourself plenty of time to get down there. It's a nice day so you should walk. In fact, if I were you, I'd pop in to the National Gallery. Look at the pictures or something. No point in being anxious. And if things really do go badly and you fail . . .' He lowered his voice and looked cautiously round the dining room. 'I failed first time myself. Silly, really, there it is. Not the end of the world. A couple of years and you never think about it.'

Campbell's afternoon examiners were sane, knowledgeable and agreeable. The traditional examiners' lunch had done its benign work, and they talked about headaches, working their way gently from the common and trivial to the rare and serious, ending up with the various catastrophes consequent upon rupture of a cerebral aneurysm. Campbell did not do too badly on the clinical features and they went on to discuss the postmortem findings. Where in the cerebral circulation did these things arise? Mainly in the circle of Willis, said a still small voice inside Campbell. He said it out loud. The examiners concurred, but pressed for further details. Commonest sites in that arterial circle? Anteriorly.

Good. There was a pause, in which Campbell knew what the next question was going to be. He rehearsed his answer and was rewarded. 'It is formed by the anterior communicating, the anterior cerebral, the posterior communicating and the posterior cerebral and basilar arteries.' One of the examiners looked at the other as though a pet theory about modern membership candidates had just bitten the dust.

They went on to discuss the management of a suspected case of tuberculosis. Perhaps by now fatalistic, Campbell said what he would have done in real life: ask one of the remaining specialists in that disappearing disease to review the case. The examiner who had not asked the question laughed, and the two of them discussed the point, virtually ignoring Campbell, until the invigilator's bell signalled the end.

That evening, mindful of Creech's advice on forgetting all about the exam until the list of successful candidates went up, Campbell went for a drink with Hadden and Bones which turned into a surreal excursion through a pubscape with blurred figures, interrupted at one point for an Indian meal and ending in half an hour's maudlin reflection on a verandah three floors up in the Institute, outside the cardiothoracic surgery department. Bones's staff nurse sent out coffee and sandwiches, and they sat looking out across the courtyard far below to the hills and the southern sky.

The night was mild and the metal verandah, its walkways and platforms surrounded by ventilation trunking and softly humming machinery, conveyed somehow the impression of the boatdeck of a ship sailing mysteriously across a night sea. Hadden, Bones and Campbell drank coffee in its sheltered warmth and talked about other travellers through time and medicine: their skill and luck, their strengths and failings, their sex lives and their job prospects, their albatrosses and their great saves.

At eleven the staff nurse, in the nicest possible way, indicated that it might be better if they went. Hadden stumped off down the upper surgical corridor. Bones said something about going back to the flat. Campbell did not accompany him, but went instead to the residency to see Jo, who had not been expecting him but made him welcome. The telephone call that interrupted them could have been better timed, but since she was on call for the ward Jo was half expecting it. As she listened her face changed suddenly in genuine surprise, then she smiled. 'It's for you.'

'Me?'

She gave him the telephone.

'Well, young Campbell, I've been ringing your flat every half hour for the last two hours.' It was Bertram.

'Sorry. I was out.'

'So I gathered. Then I learned from your flatmate, also pissed out of his head, that this might be a good number to try.'

'Oh.'

'It's unofficial. But definite.'

'What?'

'You've passed.'

'Passed?'

'Very scrapey. But you made it.'

'Oh. Thanks.'

'You lucky bugger.'

'Gosh. Thanks.'

Campbell put the phone down and shouted, 'I did it.' He had not meant to shout, but he was drunk and surprised and he had just passed membership. Jo put a finger to her lips. Through the wall adjoining the bed came an angry triple knock. Campbell and Jo both laughed, as quietly as they could in the circumstances, and hugged each other.

'Who's that?'

'Betty somebody. Works in ward twenty-three. Very god squad. Thinks I'm awful.'

'Sorry.'

Jo giggled again and moved a little, taking care not to dislodge Campbell. 'I told you you'd pass.'

'I didn't think I had.'

'Aren't you clever?'

'Did I tell you I missed a spleen?'

'Yes. Twice. But it doesn't matter now.'

135

'I suppose not . . . But it's a bit worrying. Somebody at the Southern says standards are falling.'

'That's what Barry says.'

'Does he?'

'You must have been really clever about the rest of it.'

'Maybe. Gosh. I've passed.'

With her left heel Jo drew slow gentle circles on Campbell's right buttock. New vistas opened. The Neurobiology Unit had done for Campbell all that he had asked of it. Chief Backstay, who could be telephoned in the morning, might have a frigate bound for the West Indies, or one of the survey ships, which were said to offer, by the standards of the service, a life of luxury and leisure. The circles became smaller and more insistent. There remained the question of how soon Campbell might decently disentangle his fortunes from those of Dr Brown.

Jo moved her right leg, curling a foot between Campbell's thighs, then tensed under him, lifting him a few inches and holding him there while expertly modulated waves of tension rippled away towards resolution.

'Are you going to leave Bobby's unit?'

'Probably.'

'And go back to the navy?'

'Yes. Probably.'

'Can I go on top now?'

'Fine.'

Jo stayed on top for twenty minutes or so, sometimes smiling, sometimes thoughtful, always considerate and relaxed, occasionally murmuring gratefully or contentedly, her hair swinging around her breasts and her hands roving over Campbell's chest, neck and shoulders. He lay under her, also considerately in control, contemplating his various good fortunes. He had passed the exam and would very soon become a Member of the Royal College of Physicians. He had heard the news in unusual but far from unpleasant circumstances, having put Bertram, his mentor, to some trouble in the business of finding him, though that scarcely mattered.

'Now I'm going to finish you off.'

Jo did, in a way that reminded Campbell of something a

brother officer had once said in speculation about a girl at a wardroom cocktail party: a vivid naval phrase about sex, that he could not recall in detail.

Jo sighed and flopped moistly over him, her head on his left shoulder. He reached for the bedlight and switched it off. As usual, Jo fell asleep instantly. Campbell, knowing he could not sleep like that, but feeling it somehow discourteous to slide out from under too promptly, lay waiting as her breathing deepened. A little longer, and he could move without waking her. The elusive naval phrase came at last to mind. 'She'd squeeze you till the wax popped out of your ears.' Campbell giggled. Jo stirred and slid off him, without quite waking.

As Campbell lay on the outside half of the single bed waiting for sleep, the door opened, throwing a wedge of light from the corridor into the room and across the bed. No one had knocked. The door had simply opened. Someone stood for a moment before retreating, just as quietly, into the corridor, and closing the door. Male, thin, above average height. There had been an indistinct glimpse of profile as the intruder had turned. That, with something about the ears and hair-line, had been enough to identify the house officer's late-night visitor as their colleague, Dr Barry Swift.

Campbell, shaken suddenly from his drunk and drowsy post-membership euphoria, was surprised, then, when he had thought about it, he realized that he should not have been. One or two things Jo had said about Barry at various times, her amused tolerance of his oddity on the wards and, most of all, her exceedingly direct, practical and unemotional approach to matters sexual should all have prepared him for something like this, although the exact timing could have been kinder.

When Jo was deeply asleep, Campbell got up, dressed and departed, wondering momentarily if he ought to leave a note to that effect on the door for Barry. He decided against it, and left the residency quietly, hoping not to bump into anyone as he did so. As he walked across the park to Marchmont, it began to rain.

* * *

Next morning, Chief Backstay was apologetic. Sir had just missed a very nice number, a survey ship as it happened, going to some islands in the South Atlantic that were very nice at this time of year. And there was something in the wind for Malta, also nice at this time of year, in hospital medicine, but nothing definite yet. Perhaps later. Campbell mentioned his examination pass. Chief said that the bloke in Malta liked that sort of thing, but there wasn't actually a billet just yet. However, he would keep in touch.

Campbell was disappointed. He put the phone down and sat looking out across the Institute's lawn to the clock tower. If he had no job to go to, the matter of leaving the Neurobiology Unit was less urgent. The post in the naval hospital in Malta sounded interesting, but was, so far, far too indefinite to act on. The best thing to do might be to hang on for a few weeks more, a study job being, after all, more of a holiday than a job once you had passed whatever you were studying for. The arrangement with Dr Brown had made no mention of notice to quit, but perhaps a week would be about right when something turned up. Meantime, he would stay on.

He was still staring out of the window when Fiona came in.

'Your ten o'clock man rang in to say he wasn't coming.'

'Oh?'

'Have you got a hangover?'

'Yes.'

'Want a coffee?'

'Thanks. Why isn't he coming?'

'Stopped the tablets. Found out it was research, and somebody in a pub told him that medical research was bad for you. Could damage your health. So he's stopped the tablets and he's not coming in. A Mr Girdwood.'

'Fine by me.'

'Sugar?'

'No thanks.'

Three weeks elapsed. Chief Backstay did not ring back. Campbell, who had been passing exams on and off for about twenty years, found his elation at passing membership short-lived. Perhaps because there were now no more exams to pass, life seemed less straightforward than it had been before. The activities of the Neurobiology Unit, which had never fully engrossed his attention, now occupied only a few hours of each day. Having little to do, he found his sketchy inessential duties on the wards irksome and unrewarding. With Hadden, now a lecturer with senior registrar status, and Bones, who had also just passed the last exam of his life, he spent more and more time in pubs.

The Edinburgh autumn progressed to chill and early darkness, so that the prospect of a week in Rhodes, even one spent talking about Auragen, seemed less unattractive. More patients dropped out of the trial. In far-off Rumania, two septuagenarian party stalwarts attained cabinet rank in a reshuffle precipitated by the deaths of two nonagenarians, the senior of whom, the *Economist* assiduously reported, was reputed to have died in the arms of his thirty-one-year-old mistress.

PART FOUR

'You never met Theresa's parents, David, did you?'

'No. I really hardly knew her.'

'Remarkable couple.'

'Really? I never met them.'

'Really remarkable. Especially her father. Ever heard of Monte Cassino, David?'

'Is that in Italy?'

'Italy. That's right. He was there.'

'Theresa's father?'

'Yes . . . Remarkable chap.'

'So you were saying.'

'Yes. Hellish business.'

'Oh. In the war?'

'Right, David. Hellish business.'

'And he was in it? In the army, I suppose.'

'Right, David. The Polish army.'

'Of course.'

'They walked there, you know.'

'The Poles?'

'Yes. Thousands of them. Thousands of miles. Halfway across Russia and through Turkey.'

'To Italy?'

'Well, yes. Eventually. And Cassino was what it was all about. On a hill. And the Poles took it. Terrific casualties. A sort of death ride, and Theresa's father was there. Remarkable chap. A cavalry officer. But they were walking by then. And they got shot to bits.'

'You met him, this chap?'

'Yes. That's what I was going to say. He was a very bright historian. Then the war came. So into the cavalry. Then infantry.'

'Then?'

'The Post Office.'

'Really?'

'Yes. Hadn't quite finished his PhD when the war came. Full of shrapnel when it ended. So . . . the Post Office. A lot of Poles like that in Edinburgh. Mathematicians and philosophers running tuppenny-ha'penny tobacconists. Sad, really. And broken, really broken, when she died . . . Saw them about a couple of months ago, when I took round those things from her office. The old chap sat like . . . like a general. "She voz our hope," he said. "She voz our hope . . ." She was, you know. A tragic business.'

'Tragic.' Campbell had been wondering how Dr Brown had come to meet the parents of the late Dr Jankowska. The little silver propelling pencil which he had passed on to Fiona with a view to somehow getting it back to them must have gone by hand of consultant.

'I'd met them before, of course.'

'Really?'

'Yes. The old lady's remarkable too.'

'Polish?'

'Oh yes. And a fine old lady. Been in a labour camp somewhere. By the time the Americans got there half of them were dead. Came to Scotland because she thought Stashek might have ended up there.'

'Stashek?'

'The old chap.'

'I see.'

'Terrible business.'

'But she found him?'

'Yes . . . I meant Theresa. She should have lived. She should be here. Now.' Dr Brown said that with childlike

141

drunken conviction. Campbell said, 'Sad business.'

'You don't mind me talking like this, David?'

'Not at all.'

'It really rocked me.'

'Yes . . . I gather she was very good.'

'Irreplaceable . . .' Dr Brown rolled a miniature bottle between his hands, inverted it over his glass and was rewarded with two or three drops of brandy. Campbell's whisky, his third of the flight, was low but not exhausted. He ran it round the glass, so that little fingers of fluid climbed the sides.

'Another, David?'

'Um . . . no thanks.'

'It's all on Kristall Morgen. Or possibly the airline. Sure?'

'Thanks. Well, maybe a tonic or a soda water or something, if you're having another.'

Dr Brown had rung for a stewardess before Campbell had finished the sentence. They were somewhere over the Eastern Mediterranean, and eight hours behind schedule. The UK contingent to the symposium on the management of the dementias had arrived at Gatwick only to be told that the flight had been delayed by industrial action at their destination. Rhodes was still an hour away in the darkness, their new time of arrival shortly after midnight. In the hours at Gatwick Campbell had gone over his presentation several times, glad of the extra time for its preparation. Most of the others had killed time in bars and restaurants.

'Sir?' A stewardess with a tired, well-trained smile had appeared.

'Another, thank you. And a soda water, David?'

'Thanks.'

'Ice?' Dr Brown asked.

'Yes, thanks.'

'I'm sorry, sir . . .'

'Fine. Just a soda water.'

The girl went off. Dr Brown turned to Campbell. 'You're single, David?'

'Yes.'

'Footloose and fancy free?'

142

'More or less.' Dr Brown had no particular need to know about the private lives of his junior medical staff.

'Thinking about settling down?'

'Only in very general terms.'

'Ah, yes. . . Thanks, lass. . .' Dr Brown opened his fourth miniature brandy with much the same enthusiasm as he had the first. Campbell added some soda water to his whisky. 'Sorry about the ice, sir. But if you'd like another whisky . . .'

'No thanks. This is fine.'

The girl, a pale blonde, looked exhausted. In the oval of darkness to his left Campbell could make out half a dozen stars and a wing, silver in the moonlight, juddering sometimes in minor turbulence. His talk for the symposium was, so far as it could be, ready: a ten-minute outline of the work with word-pairing tests in patients on high and low doses of Auragen. He had eight slides, and another two, the crucial ones with data from results taken over and processed in Hamburg, would, it was promised, be ready and waiting for him in Rhodes.

Dr Brown seemed to want to go on talking. He coughed and said, 'What do you see yourself doing five years from now, David?'

'Hm.' The question seemed to Campbell to arise from a melancholy inebriation rather than from any detailed interest in his future welfare. He sipped his whisky and soda and said, 'Don't know. Depends what comes up.' Chief Backstay had still not rung back.

'Don't leave it too late.'

'No.'

'I got a fright at forty.'

'Really?'

'A real fright. I had a consultant job, a hundred publications, a house and a car. And that was it.'

'I see.'

'It's very easy to let that happen, David. To do virtually nothing but medicine. Very easy indeed. Patients, time in the lab, time in the library, and things like this.'

'I suppose so,' said Campbell without conviction.

'The pay-off, of course, is the chair.'

'Of course.'

Dr Brown smiled and sighed. 'It's not generally appreciated . . . but one can do so much more as a professor. The title's fine, and the academic politics . . . Well, I've seen enough of that as a senior lecturer. But grants, projects, staff . . . all these things really become just a whole lot simpler. Whether you like it or not, it's a fact of life. So interview fourth of October, a couple of months of bureaucratic messing about . . . and then . . .'

That seemed to Campbell to incorporate a large assumption about the relative fortunes of Dr Brown and the principal outside contender: an assumption not shared by some knowledgeable observers. He glanced out at the moonlit wing and the stars.

'I think everything's going to be all right.' Dr Brown sniffed the brandy in his unconnoisseurlike clear plastic beaker. 'I had thought we were cutting it a bit fine . . . you know . . . with the Auragen results breaking, and the timing of the major publications. But everything looks as if it's going to be all right now. Sinclair might as well stuff his miserable sixty or so papers up his arse and hang about for somewhere like Leicester or Melbourne.' He took a large sip of brandy. 'But Theresa should have been here to see it . . . And share it, David. And share it.'

Campbell was astonished, but said nothing. If Dr Brown had had serious ideas of that sort about the late Dr Jankowska, then his social judgement was simply awful. The notion was ludicrous and embarrassing, though it had to be admitted that stranger couples did exist. Campbell looked out of the window. It was not only a question of social judgement. The same ghastly flaw ran through Dr Brown's thinking in clinical and scientific matters too. The man who would be professor could not distinguish the real from the unreal. There was a long silence.

'So don't sacrifice too much to medicine, David. Don't leave things too late.'

'No.'

'What about that house officer, David? The wee girl from Manchester? But I shouldn't be giving you ideas you haven't had for yourself. Not in that department. And I'd really appreciate it if what I've said about poor Theresa goes no farther . . . You sure you don't fancy a whisky? A night cap?'

The plane touched down at half past midnight. Its passengers waited on board for another hour while those from four other planes, all delayed by a ground-staff strike which had ended at midnight, cleared immigration and customs. Dr Brown, quiet after his strange divulgence, sat dozing, then stood sleepily in front of Campbell in a bad-tempered queue for immigration checks and another for customs. Outside the terminal building by 2 a.m., they were met by a thin, dark man who spoke no English but carried a large sign with the Kristall Morgen logo and 'Auragen Symposium'. He led them to a bus, then drove them ten miles along a bumpy coastal road to their hotel, where a sleepy porter cursed their baggage in Greek. By the time they collected their room keys Dr Brown had revived a little. 'Good night, David. What's left of it. Pity we missed the champagne reception and the opening dinner, but they'll probably have something just as good tomorrow. Good night.'

'I don't know about all those tests, but we've certainly noticed a considerable improvement.'

'Considerable improvement.'

'Ian feels generally much more alert, and is enjoying a lot more things than he did when he was ill. He's watching *much* more television.'

'Much more television.'

'And we're terribly grateful to Bobby and everybody at the Neurobiology Unit. Everyone's been terribly kind. And I've been meaning to say, Dr Campbell . . . I didn't really get a chance at the airport or on the plane . . . I've been meaning to talk to you, so I hope you don't mind us joining you . . .'

'Not at all.'

'You probably thought me a bit . . . brusque . . . the first time we met. You remember. At the Unit. I think I was a bit nervous, because of Ian's illness, at that stage. And you were

145

very kind. You can understand that, I'm sure. You must see a lot of anxious relatives.'

'Anxious relatives.'

'One or two,' said Campbell. The grapefruit segments were tinned and might have been opened longer than was good for them.

'We've become quite interested in the whole business. It turns out the condition's quite common and Ian's been only too glad to refer people up to Bobby's clinic so that they can benefit too.'

Dr Duke looked as if he were about to say something, but his wife raised a hand to silence him, and continued to talk herself, taking quick, birdlike sips at some dubious tomato juice as she did so. 'And out of the blue came an invitation to this symposium. Bobby's terribly *good* at that sort of thing. Terribly good.'

'Terribly good.'

'And I've been hearing that he's practically certain to get the chair. Not just be head of neurobiology, but the whole department.'

Campbell laid aside his grapefruit and lifted his coffee cup, nodding vaguely as he did so.

'With Ian's being ill we didn't really manage a holiday this summer so we thought it would be quite nice to slip away somewhere. Combining it with work, of course. And as I was saying, Ian's become terribly interested in this sort of thing.'

'This sort of thing.' Dr Duke was eating breakfast cereal, using his fingers to push it onto the spoon. Mrs Duke reached over and restrained the offending hand. 'How's your room, Dr Campbell? Does it look out to sea?'

Campbell shook his head and continued to sip his coffee.

'They've probably put the . . . senior people in the nicer rooms. We had a wonderful view this morning. Quite the sort of thing you come to a place like this for. The sun rising, literally coming straight out of those mountains over there. Yugoslavia, is it, dear? You were somewhere near here in the war, weren't you, dear? Yugoslavia?'

'Yugoslavia,' said Dr Duke.

'Really, Dr Campbell, we've noticed such a difference.'

*   *   *

In a jungle of huge rubber plants in the foyer, two tall blonde girls stood by a table with rows and rows of name badges. A loose queue advanced to be recognized and submit to a little ceremony of investiture in which the officiating girl smiled and said, with a vaguely Scandinavian accent, 'Welcome. What is your name, please? Yes, of course. We are expecting you. Welcome,' pinned the appropriate badge to the noviTiate and then handed over a glossy folder labelled, like many other objects in sight, 'Auragen Symposium'. Campbell waited between a clump of solid-looking men in cheap double-breasted suits, presumably part of the Rumanian delegation, and three girls, American from the sound of them, and therefore probably representing the Tijuana group. One was telling the other two that they should have known there were a lot of strikes in Europe, and that the meeting should have been held in San Diego instead.

There was more coffee in the foyer and Campbell, duly badged and with his folder under his arm, moved across to join a lesser queue. The symposium seemed to have attracted between forty and fifty participants. In addition to Dr Brown, Dr and Mrs Duke and Campbell, the Edinburgh contingent included Campbell's erstwhile classmate, Dr Able (who had, after all, expressed a firm intention of qualifying by a policy of enthusiastic referral), another, rather quieter general practitioner, and Kristall Morgen's local representative, the increasingly irksome Mike Forrest, who had got thoroughly drunk early on at Gatwick and slept for most of the subsequent wait and all of the flight.

Dr Brown was at that moment secluded in the undergrowth of the rubber-plant jungle with Dr Lundquist, the medical director of Kristall Morgen and one of the two company plenipotentiaries who had visited Edinburgh at the height of the data-handling crisis. Lundquist, tall and a little overweight, pale and grey-eyed, had listened a lot and said little. His colleague on that visit, a short, tubby German who had talked a little more, mainly to agree with Dr Brown and promise generous remedial action, was standing, alone and not a little shifty, at the edge of the crowd, like a theatre manager before a doubtful first night.

147

In the event it was he who, at ten precisely, opened the swing doors marked 'Auragen Symposium: Main Conference Room' and ushered people in. Inside, the layout seemed to Campbell, with little experience of either it was true, more appropriate to a press conference than a scientific meeting. A podium, covered in a shiny gold foil of the kind in which the drug under study was wrapped, was furnished with a similarly covered table and lectern, the latter complete with microphone, light, projector control, the usual 'Auragen Symposium' signs and the Kristall Morgen logo. Above hung a large film screen and two video monitors.

Drs Lundquist and Brown waited at the back with a short, vaguely familiar man while the rest of the participants found seats and settled down. A couple of photographers appeared from nowhere and the trio at the back came forward, mounting the little dais amid a blitz of flashbulbs. The Eastern Mediterranean Symposium on the Management of the Dementias had begun.

Dr Lundquist, large and solemn, took up position behind the lectern and waited a few seconds while another fusillade of flash photography subsided. He spoke slowly, in almost accentless English, and said little that was unexpected, welcoming the participants, regretting the previous night's inconvenience to them and dwelling at some length on his admiration for their scientific interest in the diseases under discussion. The Rumanians, increasingly lost since he had said good morning, frowned in puzzlement, then settled to boredom. In Lundquist's view this symposium, to which millions looked with hope, marked the beginning of the conquest of one of the major afflictions of the civilized world. He was sure the hopes raised would not go unfulfilled. The champagne reception, scheduled for the previous evening, would now take place tonight. Excitedly, one of the Rumanians translated this last item for his colleagues.

Dr Brown was introduced as chairman of the first session, which covered the basic science involved. He too had little to say that was unexpected. He talked in praise of basic science and the relationship between medical practice and its laboratory foundations. Campbell listened with disbelief, first mild,

148

later almost vehement. Thinking of Dr Brown's laziness, mental untidiness and general gullibility, and of his own recent disillusionment by first-hand experience, he concluded that the average doctor used in his daily work about as much science as the average cook, and that a great deal of mischief, tedium and abuse arose from the pretence that it was otherwise. That decided, he recognized the short man on the platform just before Dr Brown introduced him: he was Dr Boris Engelman, head of the Kristall Morgen Cerebral Metabolism Research Laboratories at Hamburg, and scientific star of the much acclaimed movie *Auragen: the Answer*.

Campbell switched off. Engelman, even more incomprehensible in the flesh than on the screen, talked quickly and showed slides, going through his knit-your-own-memory-restorer routine at considerably greater length. The audience was lost and bored but that, in the context, was the role of science: if you wanted to reduce doctors to a state of commercially exploitable quiescence, you showered them with information they did not understand and then flattered them by pretending that you thought they understood it. Your flattery made them dishonest. Their dishonesty made them gullible. Their gullibility induced them to prescribe whatever you were selling, especially if the whole process took place in circumstances which made full allowance for their avarice, gluttony and taste in liquor.

'And so . . .' said Dr Engelman, much as he had done in the film '. . . we have . . .' he paused '. . . dithiopenta-phosphatebisergolamide.' This was, after all, a scientific meeting. 'But to make the life easier for all of us, we call it Auragen.'

Dr Engelman's paper prompted nothing in the way of comment or questions from the floor. Dr Brown exercised the traditional role of the chairman in the circumstances and produced a bland, almost subservient query about a similar but previously discarded compound. The point dealt with, he went on to compare the speaker with such giants of chemotherapy as Ehrlich, at which Dr Engelman nodded politely. Dr Brown, pudgy and glutinously sincere, recorded his appreciation of what he described as a masterly presentation of a brilliant piece of molecular engineering. Two of the audience rose to leave.

Outside, a couple of faded palm trees rustled in a sea breeze. Campbell, tired and uncomfortable after the journey and a short, restless night, settled farther into his chair and consulted the symposium programme again. The next speaker was Professor Dr Elena Lupescu, of the Rumanian State Institute of the Neurological Sciences, Bucharest. She was short and bosomy and wore a black wig like a dead crow. In her progress towards the podium she passed close by, leaving a pungent invisible trail with hints of, among other things, kippers and cheap soap powder. Too short and stout to negotiate the steps unassisted with any dignity, she was raised up by the gallant arm of Dr Brown. Simply from the way they smiled at each other, Campbell concluded that her contribution to the morning's deliberations would be tedious, pretentious and most probably fraudulent.

He was not disappointed. Her first five minutes' worth consisted of enthusiastic but barely intelligible tributes to the chemical wizardry of Dr Engelman and the organizing genius of her current chairman, to whom she repeatedly referred as Professor Dr Brown of Edimburg. Dr Brown, far from being embarrassed by this, smiled quietly round the audience, though somehow avoiding Campbell's eye as he did so.

Professor Lupescu, or more likely a lowly collective of her laboratory staff, had taken brains from healthy young rats and done a number of things to them that would have rendered them even less like those of the patients being given the drug in real life, and measured with suspicious accuracy the uptake by them of tiny amounts of a substance thought by some workers to have something to do with the chemical basis of memory. To no one's surprise, the addition of just a dash of dithiopentophosphatebisergolamide greatly facilitated this process. QED, and another triumph for socialist realism and the Rumanian rat-brain industry, thought Campbell, as one of the men in cheap suits rose with a camera to record the moment for posterity. At least the girl sitting beside him, one of the Americans, smelt nice and had the good sense to appear unimpressed.

150

On the way out to coffee he got a chance to read her name badge, and on the way back in they talked briefly. She was called Lisa Dorfmann and she had taken orange juice instead of coffee because she had never been so jet-lagged in her life.

After the interval the group reassembled slowly and incompletely, with only about twenty of an audience for a man from Aix-en-Provence who talked rapidly in French for about half an hour, his only concession to the anglophone conventions of international science being a hundred-word summary read in an accent so execrable it sounded deliberate. He claimed to have shown that dithiopentophosphatebisergolamide prolonged oxygen uptake in the brains of rats judiciously reduced to a state of coma by hydrogen cyanide, from which it followed that the substance under test could also be expected to exert a protective effect on compromised neural tissue in ageing humans. To Campbell, the logic of that seemed if anything worse than the accents in which it had been delivered, but Dr Brown and several of the Rumanians, visibly led by Professor Lupescu, nodded with enthusiasm. In the course of a brief discussion of the paper Dr Brown referred to preliminary results from his own work with glucose uptake methods, unfortunately not quite ready for presentation, which tended to confirm this effect. The Frenchman scowled and resisted this suggestion, perhaps simply on grounds of anglophobia. The symposium broke for lunch a little ahead of schedule.

'Their leatherwork's quite nice. And they have little pottery things. Not really ancient Greek, but all right for ashtrays.'

'And the wine.'

'And strikes.'

'I thought the colonels had put a stop to all that.'

'You're thinking of Turkey.'

'No. Greece.'

'Greece?'

'Yes.'

'Why Greece?'

'Well, Rhodes is part of Greece.'

'Really? Well, that explains the funny writing.'

151

'And the weather's meant to be better than this. I looked it up.'

'Third this year, actually. My accountant prefers me to take this sort of holiday. And you?'

'I just rang Mike Forrest. How many patients is the Rhodes trip worth, I said. So here I am. But the town's rubbish.'

'French? No problem.'

'I don't think they have colonels any more.'

'That's what I meant. So they have strikes.'

'Much easier than that Rumanian woman, in fact. The biochemical jargon's practically identical to English once you've cracked French itself.'

'Occasional sudden death, I'd heard.'

'We'd call that a lager.'

'Really?'

'His back again. Three weeks. We very nearly couldn't come.'

'Your Heathrow is, like, the pits.'

'Libido as well as potency.'

'And your country, does it have a State Institute of Neurological Science?'

'More like a Budweiser, I guess, but OK.'

'Mainly in Puerto Rico.'

'Sunny and mid-seventies . . . huh.'

'Well, *she* thinks he's better.'

'They're more or less always difficult about that, but especially if you've claimed for everything else already.'

'And did you see the state of her fingernails?'

'Nobody under sixty, I'd heard. So they're not too worried. Yet.'

'Well, David . . . all set for Wednesday?'

'I've done what I can. Methods and all that. But it's a bit odd not actually knowing yet what came out of it.'

'Ah yes. That's one of the beauties of the double-blind controlled bit. All is revealed when you break the dose code . . . Hamburg may be a wee bit slow, but they really couldn't

152

have been more helpful with data handling once they actually appreciated what we were up against in Edinburgh. Literally half the Auragen assessment patients in the world. No wonder poor old Dr Frank had problems . . .'

'So what about the results?'

'Yes . . . yes, indeed. I'm not sure whether they're here already or whether they're coming in later today or tomorrow. But I understand from Oskar Kallmeyer that they're very, very exciting.'

'Kallmeyer?'

'Yes. The chap who came over with Lundquist. You know him. Lunch at Denzler's. In overall charge of new product data handling. And I understand he's *very* pleased with your work.'

'Oh.'

'So we're all very much looking forward to your little paper on Wednesday. What did you think of this morning's session?'

'Interesting . . . But I'm afraid my French wasn't really up to that third chap.'

'I had some difficulty myself. I practically always do with Provençals. Not what they taught us at school. But a very sound piece of work. Corroborates everything I'm finding with the glucose uptake thing. I only wish now I'd tried a lot harder to run the whole international thing by telephone from Edinburgh and spent a lot more time in the lab. That chap got most of it right but some of the things he said about ketolase activity were a bit strange, even allowing for the accent. Still, one can only do so much from the chair, and there's the diplomatic angle to be thought of. But a sound morning's work, taken altogether, I thought. A good solid basis for the clinical stuff still to come. How's your room?'

'All right. Quiet. At the back, overlooking the swimming pool.'

'Second floor?'

'Yes.'

'David . . . just in case I have to get in touch with you . . . what number?'

'Number?'

'What number's your room?'

153

'Two one eight.'

Dr Brown noted that down on the corner of a paper napkin, which he tore off and put in his pocket. 'Is that the kalamaraki?'

'Yes.'

'How is it?'

'Fine. And that?'

'Local specialty. Egg and lemon soup. Then I'm having the chicken Kiev. One should only make so many concessions to native tastes, and this is supposed to be a first-class international hotel. A little wine with that, David?'

Lunch, served in a pleasant first-floor room looking out to sea, was a distinct improvement on breakfast, and the weather too had brightened. No working session was planned for the afternoon, only a two-hour coach tour round the island, compliments of Kristall Morgen. Over coffee, Campbell looked around the room and decided against the coach trip. After lunch he went up to his room and lay for an hour reading, the pleasures of books other than medical texts still fresh after membership, then looked at the maps of town and island, also provided courtesy of Kristall Morgen, and then, at around three o'clock, wandered out on his own, going nowhere in particular. Only after three hundred yards or so and several strange glances from passers-by did he think to remove the large lapel badge which had labelled him 'Auragen Symposium' since just after breakfast.

The seafront road led round a promontory then past a series of hotels, older and less grand than the Poseidon, to the harbour and eventually to the old, walled town, in front of which an arcaded building, once a Turkish headquarters, shared a few hundred yards of waterfront with a Greek Orthodox cathedral and a bronze memorial to the liberating Allied forces of 1945. The season was over, pleasure boats moored idle, souvenir stalls closed, the pavement cafés shuttered or scarcely patronized. An old man sat on a bollard fishing, his line in clear, unpromising water close to the shore. Idle in the sun, he nodded and smiled as Campbell passed.

Beyond the first gate of the old town a steep cobbled court-yard rose towards an inner fortification, through which another, smaller gate led onto the town square. Campbell ignored the thickets of postcard racks and the café tables, vaguely in search of a bank but happier to go on exploring than to risk asking for directions. Eventually he found one, where two cashiers discussed his Royal Bank of Scotland ten-pound notes at some length before handing over a grubby and colourful bunch of local notes in exchange.

Away from the waterfront and the square, little streets and alleys, cobbled and irregular, formed a maze of more complexity than Campbell's map seemed to allow. He pocketed it and simply wandered, past butchers' and bakers' and tailors' and little dwellings whose front doors opened straight into cluttered parlours with lace and pot plants. Old ladies with headscarves and shopping bags stood at corners. There were hardly any cars and little children played unsupervised, the more daring practising their English ('Ello mister').

Open spaces were rare, dead ends commoner than in most towns, usually where a lane wound suddenly to a halt against the huge yellowish stones of the outer wall of the town. A little mosque, padlocked and decayed, its minaret ringed with dried weeds, occupied the highest ground within the walls, and from its overgrown courtyard Campbell looked back down across the jumble of roofs to the harbour, where two small naval patrol craft lay alongside a jetty, with a white cruise ship, from the Eastern Bloc to judge from its red-striped funnel, dwarfing them from behind.

It would have been interesting and perhaps easier to walk back along the top of the outer rampart, but no obvious way up to it presented itself, and Campbell made his way back through the little streets again, heading vaguely for the main square. A larger mosque, neatly painted and surrounded by a grove of small fruit trees, appeared still to be in use, and he approached its main door cautiously, as befitted a lapsed Presbyterian. An old man in baggy clothes and a skull cap saw him and beckoned him onward. He was sitting on a low bench by the door, in front of which there were two straggling rows of shoes, slippers and sandals. Campbell sat down and removed his shoes and added them to one of the rows then went inside.

The size and proportions of the building were those of an average village church at home, the atmosphere perhaps a little less severe. The walls, brilliant matt white, were liberally hung with carpets and the floors were thick with them: delicately patterned, soft and overlapping, mainly in reds, blues and purples. There were no seats, indeed no furniture of any kind other than a slender pulpit which seemed taller than was strictly necessary, and a couple of cabinets in which holy texts were displayed. A dozen or so men sat cross-legged on the floor. No formal service was in progress and no one appeared at all perturbed by the intrusion of an infidel.

In the circumstances, Campbell did not feel as uncomfortable as he would have expected, though perhaps he would have felt better had he not had a small hole at the toe of his left sock. He stood for a moment looking round, then walked over to one of the cabinets to take a closer look at one of the books. Its decorated Arabic text, beautiful and utterly obscure, might have been anything from decades to centuries old, its paper yellowing, its binding pale leather.

To stand in one's socks in the bright silence of a mosque that probably hadn't changed much in five hundred years seemed to help in getting the morning's session into perspective. Auragen, if by any chance it was any good, would prove itself over the next couple of years by gaining acceptance among doctors not paid or bribed to prescribe it. If it did not, it would become as if it had never been, in company with thousands of other equally enthusiastically trumpeted drugs of the last thirty years. The only continuing unease concerned its safety: had it actually killed people, and if so how many? And how many more might it kill before it was finally either forgotten or withdrawn? Campbell thought of the little old lady who had died in church, and of old Mrs Spence, and then of how Dr Brown had reacted when he had been told about them. He decided. Job or no job, he would resign as soon as he got back to Edinburgh.

The old man by the door handed Campbell his shoes and clearly expected a tip. The smallest denomination of note available delighted him greatly. Whatever it was, Campbell knew it was money well spent. He felt better already.

156

Although the sun was lower, the sky had cleared and the afternoon become positively warm. Campbell took off his jacket, slung it over his shoulder and sauntered down a broad street lined with shops and stalls and restaurants. As he paused to look in a furrier's window a svelte young man rushed out and tried, in English, to sell him a deerskin coat. ('As you see, very very elegant . . . and for you at a very very low end-of-season price.') Campbell heard him out and declined politely, getting a distinct impression that the man would have been astonished had he done anything else. A few stalls farther on he bought four postcards, including one of a priapic neoclassical figurine which might have amused an intending sex therapist, then farther down he stopped again, this time for coffee at a corner café whose dozen tables, all except two empty, were shaded by a large tree and offered a diverting view of the little crossroads market.

The cup of coffee was tiny, dark and sludgy, but appealing in its way, and came with a glass of water. Campbell drank both quite quickly and sat back. The waiter, a lop-sided ancient with bad osteoarthritis, hobbled over again. 'You like?'

'Yes, thank you. Another, please.'

'I bring one more.'

Over the second coffee Campbell wrote postcards to Bones, Hadden, and, after some thought, to Jo, then sat in the sun looking and listening. Two new groups had arrived at the café: one of squat, middle-aged men in old-fashioned clothes, speaking an unknown, possibly Slavic language, the other younger and much noisier, a group, so far as could be judged from fragments of conversation about Athens, Greece and the like, of American students on some kind of cultural safari. The Eastern Europeans got rapidly drunk on beer as the Americans became much rowdier simply on Coke. The old waiter, hard-pressed by the sudden rush of business, hobbled painfully about between.

The drunk men, presumably from the cruise ship in the harbour, got quickly drunker. Much more aware of the Americans than the Americans were of them, they appeared to be voicing among themselves crude appreciation of the students, both male and female. True, all were sufficiently lightly clad to be viewed as inviting such comment, but seemed too engrossed in one another to notice it until one particularly comely youth attracted, in his progress to and from the toilet, sufficient volume of enthusiasm for him to become aware of it. Blushing angrily, he hastened to shelter in the lee of an obese female with a brace on her teeth. Shortly after, with much noisy discussion of the bill, the Americans left.

Although the East–West cabaret was over, Campbell sat on as the sun went down, feeling happier than he had done for months. However narrowly and luckily, he had passed membership and, even if no alternative was yet in sight, he was leaving the Neurobiology Unit, with its posturings and its uncertainties and its strange monothematic isolation from medicine as a whole. With luck, Chief Backstay would once more provide. Bertram too would require to be telephoned. Something would turn up. He called the waiter over again and ordered a beer, and sat contentedly until it was time to go back to the Poseidon to get ready for the reception.

In the half dark of room 218 a red light flashed on the telephone. Campbell rang reception for the message thus announced and a marginal English speaker asked him to ring Dr Brown on extension three seven seex. He did so. Dr Brown did not sound sober.

'Ah. David. Good. You're all right, are you?'

'Fine, thanks.'

'What happened to you?'

'Well . . . nothing. I mean, I'm all right.'

'Thank God . . . It's just you weren't on the coach trip, and I wondered, well, perhaps if something had happened to you.'

'No.'

'Or if . . . It sounds silly, but I wondered if you'd had second thoughts.'

'Second thoughts?'

'About Wednesday.'

'No . . . I still haven't seen the results but . . .'

158

'Oh, don't worry about that. Kallmeyer'll have all that under control, believe me. I know him. It's just that . . . you disappeared.'

'Disappeared?'

'Well, you weren't on the coach trip.'

Campbell considered his phrasing. 'I don't actually . . . enjoy coach trips.'

'So where were you?'

'Oh. I just went for a walk.'

'You gave me a very worrying couple of hours, David.'

'Sorry. I just . . .'

'Very worrying indeed. And apart from that, David . . . Even though we're in Rhodes, we're still – you and I – very much the home team. People have to be taken care of . . . listened to . . . And we really have to work at it. Not too keen on the French myself, but that's the way it is. You're all right for tonight?'

'Fine.'

'Good, good. I'm sure you'll enjoy it. Some of these people are really keen to meet you, David.'

'Really?'

Dr Brown chuckled. 'Some of those lovelies from Tijuana. Oh, and while I'm in touch . . . Lindos.'

'Who?'

'No. Lindos is a place.'

'Here?'

'Well, near here. And there's an outing there tomorrow . . .'

'Oh.'

'I'm sure you'll enjoy it, David. And you won't actually be in the bus for very long. It's only a few miles down the coast. And I'm sure you'll appreciate, now I've explained, why it's important for you to go. The whole thing has to be . . . taken seriously. Much better for all concerned . . .'

'I see.'

'Thanks, David. See you downstairs shortly . . . Grand . . . grand.'

In the shower, Campbell began to wonder if he ought to be

159

having doubts about his planned presentation of the still
unknown results on Wednesday.

'And how long have you been with the Edinburgh
Neurobiology Unit, Dr Campbell?'

'Only a few months.'

'And before that? What was your work?'

'I was in the navy.'

'Ah. A good life for a young doctor . . . Some travel. Not
too much work perhaps.'

'That's about it.'

'For two years I was myself with the Swedish navy.'

'As a doctor?'

'As a doctor. For my National Service, I think you call it.
There was no choice. But that did not stop me enjoying it very
much.'

'Did you travel a lot?'

'Compared to yours, ours is only a little navy, and our trips
were little trips. We went to Greenock.'

'Greenock?'

'The people were very friendly. The mayor . . . You have
mayors?'

'Sort of . . . Provosts.'

'Yes, provost. At our party on the ship for the town people,
the provost called our captain, a very serious officer, Jimmy.
He may have had something to drink . . . Anyway, after this,
everyone calls the captain Jimmy. Oh yes, we enjoyed
Greenock very much. But you have been farther than
Greenock?'

'A bit.'

'A lot?'

'Quite a lot. I think I was quite lucky. South Africa . . .
Mauritius . . . Hong Kong.'

'You were very lucky, Dr Campbell. And now you settle
down?'

'That's the idea.'

'We need serious people in the evaluation of new pharmaceuticals.'

160

'I was wondering about that. Is there a Swedish group evaluating Auragen? There doesn't seem to be anyone in the programme.'

'Ah yes. That is one of our misfortunes. Unfortunately, we cannot do much of this ourselves. Much as we would like to.'

'Why not?'

'We have strange laws, which compel us to seek your help.'

'Really?'

'Our laws on new drugs are very, very stringent. So . . . our drug tests must be abroad.'

Campbell sipped his champagne. A new vision of Britain, or France or Mexico or Rumania for that matter, as a vast white-rat facility for the Swedish pharmaceutical industry emerged. It was not entirely pleasing. 'I see.'

'So we are very grateful. And we like to show our gratitude . . . Like this. And in the long run all countries, even our own, will reap the benefit.'

'And you're quite pleased with . . . the way things are going.'

'I think you could say that. As you have seen yourself this morning, Auragen produces certain remarkable effects. And your own work too, I understand . . . And also that of the Bucharest group, in psychological testing in human subjects.'

'Oh?'

'Remarkable. But we will have all the details soon enough. Have you met Professor Dr Elena?'

Campbell had hoped to have sufficient time with Dr Lundquist to raise the question of the drug's safety. Instead he was steered gently towards the short Rumanian lady, who was with Mike Forrest and laughing very loudly.

On the way in to dinner Campbell narrowly avoided being the only non-Rumanian at a table of six, then found himself sitting down instead with Mike Forrest, Dr Able and three of the girls from Tijuana. Miss Dorfmann was on his left. She asked him how he had enjoyed the trip that afternoon. He said he had gone to look at the town instead.

'You certainly missed a beautiful experience. They've got

161

everything. I mean, mountains, forests, a wonderful coastline and some truly lovely ruins.'

'Really?'

'Yeah. Greek stuff from way back. How was the town?'

'It's more recent. A lot of it from the Crusades, I think. I liked it. It's sort of cluttered and lived in. I just went for a walk, but I think there's a museum, and a lot of fortifications.'

'I guess I'm not into fortifications,' said Miss Dorfmann. There was an awkward silence, then she said, 'Do you have fortifications in Edenburg?'

'One or two. There's a castle.'

'I guess I'd heard of that.'

'Do you travel a lot?'

'Some. But this is my first trip to Europe.'

Without malice, Campbell asked, 'What do you think of it?'

She smiled. 'It's cute.' A waiter arrived with a seafood kebab starter, and another began to pour a white wine, which turned out to be the hock bottled exclusively for Kristall Morgen. Dr Able picked up his glass and held it thoughtfully for a moment. 'It's not cold enough, Mike.' The Kristall Morgen representative smiled patiently. Dr Able glanced round his dinner companions to ensure their undivided attention. 'Bloody Greeks. And I bet the red comes bloody freezing.'

In the break after dinner Campbell suddenly found Mike Forrest, to whom he had talked very little in the course of the meal, standing beside him. Both were fairly drunk.

'You don't like me, Dave, do you?'

Campbell said nothing and concentrated on what he was doing.

'You think because you've got a medical degree and I'm only a drug rep we shouldn't even be using the same pissoir, don't you?'

Campbell stifled an inclination to agree.

'Let me tell you, doc. Straight from the shoulder. It doesn't matter whether you like me or not. We still gotta work

162

together. You gotta work with us and we gotta work with you. Put it this way . . .' He shook his penis vehemently. 'We own you.'

Campbell moved over to wash his hands. The man from Kristall Morgen followed him. 'Drug companies have to work with people like you. A fact of life. We've got drugs. We need units. And when a company like Kristall Morgen needs a unit . . . it buys one, Dr Campbell, with you thrown in. So it doesn't matter whether you like us or not, Dr Campbell. We gotta work together.'

As Campbell washed his hands Forrest smiled at him in the mirror. 'Enjoy the cabaret, Dr Campbell. Compliments of Kristall Morgen.'

By the time they got back to the table the lights had been dimmed and more champagne had appeared. Able, drunker than Campbell or Forrest, had wrested a bottle from the waiter and was showing the American girls how it should be opened. 'Gently . . . It's not a bang you're after . . . more a kind of contented sigh . . .' The cork flew off with a sharp explosion and champagne flowed down into his sleeve. 'Bloody hell! Well, of course, if they're going to shake it first . . .' Campbell laughed and so did two of the girls. The waiter, commendably calm, dabbed at Able's suit with a napkin. 'I'm so sorry, sir. Of course I bring another.'

He went off and Forrest distributed the remains of the first bottle, giving Campbell far more than his share. 'Cheers, doc. Cheers, girls. Not one of your Napa Valley gripe waters this, but your actual Dom P, from France, Europe. Kristall Morgen salutes its esteemed colleagues . . . Lisa, Karen, Debbie, Bert . . . and, of course, Dave. Fill your boots, folks, and enjoy the cabaret. Also compliments of Kristall Morgen.'

The tables were arranged in a semicircle round an open space that now formed a stage. A spotlight swirled and flickered and some sound equipment made eerie testing noises. Campbell glanced round. Dr Brown, conspicuously drunk, shared a table with the Rumanian lady, whose wig was now angled back and to the right, and Drs Lundquist and Kallmeyer, both of whom seemed severely sober by comparison. Close by, the Rumanian rank and file were enjoying themselves hugely. Dr and Mrs Duke sat with some of the French group. For Dr Duke, the preparations for the floor show seemed to have some special significance. He sat peering round at a bemused alert, his wife looking correspondingly nervous.

There was a moment's total darkness, then the spotlight revealed a pale and rather underfed girl crouching almost naked in mid-floor. A sequinned green G-string, a small appendicectomy scar and two green tassles on her breasts all moved in time to the music. To judge from the reactions of the Rumanians, such sights were rare in Bucharest. They cheered and stomped and shouted ribald encouragement. Dr Brown, slumped low in his chair, his chin almost on his chest, watched and sipped champagne. Mrs Duke paid more attention to her husband than to the dancer.

The music speeded up and the girl worked her way round the edge of the space allotted to her, stomping and writhing with especial zeal as she passed the Rumanians. Perhaps because Dr Able was now dangerously drunk, she did not linger at that table, but passed close enough for her facial expression, that of a bored shopgirl possibly troubled by sinusitis, to mar the overall effect. She moved on to where Dr Duke sat, side on to his table, facing inwards to the stage.

Tempted perhaps by his age and air of docile, tweedy respectability, she proceeded to single him out for special attention, closing on him and writhing the upper part of her body so that the tassles rotated, first together then in opposite directions. Dr Duke sat impassive, much as he had done in Campbell's office at their first meeting, his face uplifted slightly in puzzlement. At his side his wife sat uncomfortably, clutching at her chair with one hand, the other moving to rest on her husband's forearm. This seemed to provoke the dancer to further efforts. She planted a naked foot on Dr Duke's knee and continued to writhe, so that the tassles whisked over his face and even ruffled his hair. Slowly he raised one hand, as though brushing away a fly, then settled again to impassivity. Thus rebuffed, the dancer retreated with a haughty flick of her tassles and completed her first routine with a comparatively demure last flourish in front of the senior table.

164

There was much Rumanian cheering, then the lights came up and more champagne appeared. Mrs Duke, perhaps with no continuing faith in her husband's hitherto exemplary conduct, rose and led him from the room, smiling good night to the recumbent Dr Brown as she went. Forrest reached over towards Campbell with a champagne bottle. 'Another wee glass, doc? Compliments of Kristall Morgen.' Campbell's vague resolve to drink no more that evening crumbled. After all, he had something to celebrate.

When Campbell awoke next morning there was a girl, naked and still asleep, lying beside him. He lay for a while trying, despite a numbing headache, to account for the various events which had led to this, then got up quietly and went to the loo. When he came back the girl had wakened and was sitting up in bed smiling. Unfortunately he could not remember her first name, so, rather self-consciously, he said, 'Good morning, Miss Dorfmann.'

Far from being offended, the girl laughed and said, 'Gee, you British. You're so formal . . . Hey, are you OK?'

'I'll live,' said Campbell, looking in a mirror.

'I guess you have tea in the morning.' Miss Dorfmann had picked up the telephone. 'Hello? Hello? Room service? OK. Well gimme room service . . . Dave, you want some orange juice, maybe?'

'Yes, thanks. And coffee, please, not tea.'

'OK, OK. Hello? Is that room service?' She ordered slowly and clearly, repeating both the items requested and the room number, then put the phone down and said, 'Be about ten minutes. You coming back to bed?'

Campbell did so and she snuggled close to him, ruffling his hair. 'You were drunk as a skunk last night . . . But kinda sweet.'

A fat motherly waitress brought them breakfast. Campbell had three cups of coffee and began to feel better. At about 9.15, so as to be in good time for the third scientific session, Miss Dorfmann got up and showered and dressed. Campbell saw her to the door. 'Um . . . thanks for . . . looking after me. Last night.'

165

She smiled. 'A pleasure, sir. Compliments of Kristall Morgen.' Campbell felt sick, and might have looked it. The girl smiled again and laid a hand on his naked shoulder. 'For services to medicine, Dr Campbell, in the evaluation of a wonderful new product. Have a nice day.'

Topped up with yet more coffee, from the trolley just outside the conference room, Campbell felt that he now had a fair chance of staying awake through the three presentations comprising the first clinical session of the symposium. Very few of the other participants were around, and when Dr Boigny as chairman called the meeting to order there were only eight people in the room. One of the Tijuana girls, in a highly polished performance making expert use of slides, spent most of her time detailing the special problems of psychological testing in illiterates, then produced inconclusive figures drawn from a series of only nineteen patients.

No discussion resulted, and a Rumanian in a crumpled grey suit, his English possibly more impenetrable by reason of an obvious hangover, reported at length on how dithiopentaphosphatebisergolamide had increased both wellbeing and libido in a series of 150 septuagenarians. His slides showed toothless peasants grinning in bathchairs, and dramatic graphs of various loosely conceived items claimed as measurable by Rumanian science.

Professor Dr Elena was not present, nor was Dr Brown. Perhaps more surprisingly, neither Dr Lundquist nor Dr Kallmeyer, both conspicuous by their sobriety the previous evening, had appeared by the time Dr Boigny announced the interval. Campbell began, in a vague, hungover way, to worry about the slides for his presentation the next day. If necessary, he decided during another half hour of Rumanian science, he would find out from reception Dr Kallmeyer's extension number and try ringing him before lunch.

Having failed to contact him, Campbell mentioned the problem to Dr Brown over prelunch drinks. Dr Brown seemed preoccupied as well as hungover, and mentioned something about some sort of flap in Hamburg perhaps holding things up.

166

'Some sort of flap?'

Dr Brown shook his head impatiently. 'I don't think myself there's anything to flap about, but there have been quite a few telephone calls back and forward this morning already . . . Tell you what, David, if nothing turns up by two, I'll ring through myself. I've dealt with them direct often enough. We'll just get the figures and you can put them up on an overhead projector, if we can lay our hands on one. Slides would look better, of course, and they might well be on this afternoon's plane. We'll see. Anyway, I'll grab Kallmeyer as soon as I can, David. Not to worry. It's a good little piece of work and well worth presenting, so we'll put something together somehow. But they do have other things on their minds this morning, I know.'

Campbell's donkey, a thin, willing beast with a rough brown coat and a few grey hairs around its muzzle, was almost at the back of the line. Ahead, a string of them wound its way up the path towards the acropolis, the riders laughing and lurching and trying to take photographs of each other and the surrounding landscape. Below curved the shore of an inlet, two thirds pale golden beach, the other third a jumble of fishermen's cottages. Clear water, patchy with submerged rocks, shaded deeper towards the open sea. Above, the line of the clifftop was interrupted by fragments of a defensive wall and the tops of the remaining columns of a series of ruined temples.

'Eez beautiful,' said the man leading the donkey.

'Very beautiful,' Campbell agreed.

The ride ended at the foot of a series of rock staircases and there was more hilarity as people dismounted and the donkeys were led away.

'Geeve me teep,' said Campbell's driver quietly but with great emotion. Campbell complied and the man shook his hand warmly. 'You OK.'

A tour guide in a headscarf and dark glasses shrilled them to order and marshalled them in front of a rock carving of a ship, reeled off dimensions, dates and the sites of comparable works elsewhere in the ancient world, then led off up the steps. It was warm but not uncomfortable, and the donkeys had done most of the work. The party emerged through a series of shadowy gatehouses on the acropolis, a vast irregular polygon of bare rock studded with classical and Byzantine ruins.

The guide, her voice agreeably diminished by the open space, pointed out an 88-metre portico, 9 metres wide, formerly with forty-two columns, built in 208 BC. The Rumanians glowered at each other in puzzlement. Campbell, happy that his modest educational needs could be met from the plan of the site included in his pocket guide, worked his way to the edge of the group and drifted off, he hoped without causing offence. In the distance, the guide warned of the danger of going too close to the edge of cliffs in places exceeding 130 metres in height.

Campbell worked his way round the landward side of the acropolis, where the cliffs dropped to dried-up pasture grazed by minute, tethered goats, and the roofs of Lindos shimmered white in the sun. To the south, the rocky platform narrowed to a point, beyond which hazy, grey-green mountains sloped to distant sea. From the point itself there was a near vertical drop of several hundred feet to a rocky shore. Campbell stood for a few minutes watching the seagulls gliding past below then moved to rejoin the rest of the group.

They had reached the forecourt of something called the temple of Lindian Athene, quite near the southern extremity of the acropolis. Campbell, approaching through the temple itself, got quite close before he noticed anything was wrong. The guide was not talking. Someone had fallen and someone else was trying to help. A man shouted, then a woman screamed: thin, high anguish fading to silence.

Campbell hurried across broken flagstones and between the remaining columns of the façade. In the centre of the group Dr Brown was kneeling over, his head almost touching that of the figure on the ground. The little huddle opened as Campbell came closer and he knelt down beside his chief.

Dr Duke lay dead and Dr Brown was trying to resuscitate him, blowing in his mouth and frantically pounding his chest.

He paused and turned to Campbell. 'I got him right away, David. Couldn't have been quicker. He should do well. I'll breathe him and you keep hitting his chest . . . He should be fine . . .' Dr Brown stooped over again. Dr Duke's head fell sideways and vomit streamed from his mouth. Dr Brown swayed and retched, then frantically wiped the vomit from the corpse's face with a grubby white handkerchief.

'What were his pupils like when you started?'

'A wee bit up. But not fixed. Definitely not fixed.'

'And now?'

'They're . . . Oh God. Just keep pounding his chest, David . . . And as soon as I've cleared his airway . . .'

Campbell stopped compressing the chest and examined the eyes for himself. Dr Duke's pupils were huge and unreactive even though he was lying in direct sunlight. They were fixed and dilated. He was dead. There was another anguished scream, very close by.

It was a long time before anything else happened. The body of Dr Duke, straightened out a little, the arms folded across the chest, lay in the sun in the forecourt of the temple of Lindian Athene while the guide went down to the ticket office beside the ship carved in the rock, where at least there was a telephone. Twenty minutes later a stout policeman sweated up the steps and across the acropolis and agreed that Dr Duke was dead. Using the guide as an interpreter he took statements from Dr Brown, Campbell and the newly widowed Mrs Duke. At around four o'clock the tourists were permitted to leave the scene.

Dr Brown helped Mrs Duke down the steps. The donkey ride back to the village was a subdued affair, the donkey drivers sullen, perhaps both awed at what had taken place and resentful of the delay and the consequent loss of business. In the bus Mrs Duke sobbed and sniffed, clutching Dr Brown's arm all the way back to the hotel. At the reception desk there were conversations about sedation, and the hotel physician and an assistant manageress shepherded Mrs Duke off towards a lift.

169

'A tragic mistake,' said Dr Brown when she had gone. 'Letting a poor old chap like that, quite unfit and over-dressed, climb a thing like that with the temperature in the high seventies. Heather should have kept him down in the taverna with Elena and old Boigny. Ian would have enjoyed that, and he would still have been here.'

Campbell recalled that he had examined Dr Duke in detail only a few months before. 'I thought he was quite fit for his age.'

'Well . . .' said Dr Brown, 'that's as may be. But there's definitely quite a strong family history of ischaemic heart disease . . . Come on, David. Let's try and get through to Hamburg again for those results. With any luck they'll have sorted themselves out after this morning's panic.'

They went up to Dr Brown's room. Getting through to the Hamburg number proved less than straightforward. Dr Brown put down the phone impatiently. 'She says ten minutes, David. She'll ring back.' He got up and walked over to the window. 'Drink, David?'

'Perhaps a small one.'

Dr Brown went over to a briefcase on the desk and pulled out a bottle of whisky. 'I'm afraid it's toothglasses.'

'That's all right.'

He poured a small whisky for Campbell and a large one for himself. Campbell said something polite and sympathetic about Mrs Duke.

'Heather'll get over it,' said Dr Brown. 'She was under a lot of strain, you know.'

'So I gathered.'

'Even though he's been getting better.'

The telephone rang and Dr Brown picked it up and said, 'Ah, thank you,' then began to talk in rapid, fluent German. There was a pause then he changed back to English again, slow and clear. 'Yes . . . The Edinburgh data gathered by Dr Campbell. And before that by Dr Jankowska . . . Yes. Dr Campbell is here with me . . . Fine. I'll wait.' He continued to listen, reaching for his drink. Campbell got up and looked out of the window.

'Hello? Yes, Dr Höss? Good. Bobby Brown here . . . Yes.

Still in Rhodes . . . Very well, thanks . . . Ah. Good. Grand. Oh? No, certainly not officially . . . No, just rumours, really. Yes . . . Yes, I agree entirely . . . Quite . . . Quite . . . No, not at all . . . Of course not . . . Be glad to . . . Thanks again, Dr Höss . . . Yes . . . Grand.'

Dr Brown put the phone down and leaned forward in his chair, clutching his brow and looking quite unwell. 'They had a meeting,' he said, 'a couple of hours ago . . . Auragen's been withdrawn.'

Campbell put down his drink. 'Safety?'

'No.' Dr Brown gave a ghostly chuckle. 'Danger.'

'Deaths?'

'One or two.' There was a silence. 'Twelve, actually.'

'Sudden deaths?'

'Yes.'

'Cardiac?'

'Yes.'

'I see.'

Dr Brown finished his drink and stood up. 'A great pity . . . And we've really never had anything that works before . . . What I'd like to do now is get back to the drawing board . . . It's a mild stimulant . . . We've always known that. What Boris Engelmann has to do now is take his magic molecule apart and see if he can put it together again without the bit that . . . that kills people. It might take a couple of years, but it's been done before. You'll probably remember the early H-2 antagonists, David. They killed people too. But look at what we've got now. And if anyone can do that Boris Engelmann can . . .' Dr Brown walked over to his briefcase again. Campbell watched as he poured another whisky, and wondered if he should wait until they were back in Edinburgh before broaching the subject of his resignation. Perhaps, in the changed circumstances, resignation would be unnecessary. In either case, it could wait a few days.

When he got back to his room a piece of paper lay where it had been pushed under the door. It was a photocopy letter, signed by Dr Lundquist, stating briefly that the compound

171

dithiopentaphosphatebisergolamide had been withdrawn on grounds of safety. Participants in the symposium were thanked for their valuable contributions in an important area of investigation. The remaining scientific session was cancelled. Travel arrangements were unchanged. The company regretted any inconvenience that had been caused.

At around six Dr Brown rang Campbell to ask whether he would like to join him for dinner in one of the restaurants in town. They met in the foyer of the Poseidon and walked along the seafront past the Turkish cemetery and up into the walled town. Dr Brown had regained a little of his composure and chatted of things other than drug evaluation.

The waiter was just removing the remains of a grilled fish entrée when a disturbance occurred near the door of the restaurant. A middle-aged woman, her hair dishevelled, her eyes red and staring, stood arguing with the head waiter. She appeared to be demanding admission, so far without success. She raised her voice and the manager and another waiter moved towards her. At this, she began to flail her arms and shriek. As she was bundled out still screaming 'Murderer, murderer,' Campbell recognized her.

'That was Mrs Duke.'

Dr Brown looked at the menu. A flashing blue light outside signified the arrival of a police car, and the disturbance came rapidly to an end. Dr Brown was still looking at the menu. 'She's been under a lot of strain recently,' he said, handing it to Campbell. 'I wonder what sedation they gave her.'

Next morning Campbell was wakened by a telephone call from the manager of the hotel. Would Dr Campbell care to come up to room 376? He got up and dressed and walked upstairs, going over in his mind the management of acute alcoholic intoxication.

Dr Brown lay in bed, and was dead rather than drunk. The manager, a poised and fluent Frenchman in a black tail coat, watched as Campbell checked for pulses that were no longer there and shone the bed light in his late chief's blank, lifeless eyes.

172

There was an empty whisky bottle on the bedside table, presumably the one that had been almost full at four the previous afternoon. On impulse Campbell checked the brief-case on the desk. In it there were three of the golden foil one-month packs of Auragen, with every blister empty of its golden tablet. As Campbell lifted them out and looked at them, the manager nodded understandingly.

'It happens, sir . . . It happens.'